ALSO BY TERENCE FAHERTY

The Quiet Woman

The Owen Keane Mysteries

Deadstick
Live to Regret
The Lost Keats
Die Dreaming
Prove the Nameless
The Ordained
Orion Rising
Eastward in Eden
The Confessions of Owen Keane

The Scott Elliott Mysteries

Kill Me Again
Come Back Dead
Raise the Devil
Dance in the Dark
The Hollywood Op

TALES OF THE STAR REPUBLIC

TALES OF THE STAR REPUBLIC

TERENCE FAHERTY

THE GISBOURNE PRESS

Cover: Cover Story Design

Interior Design: Sue Trowbridge, interbridge.com

Print ISBN: 978-0-692-72988-5

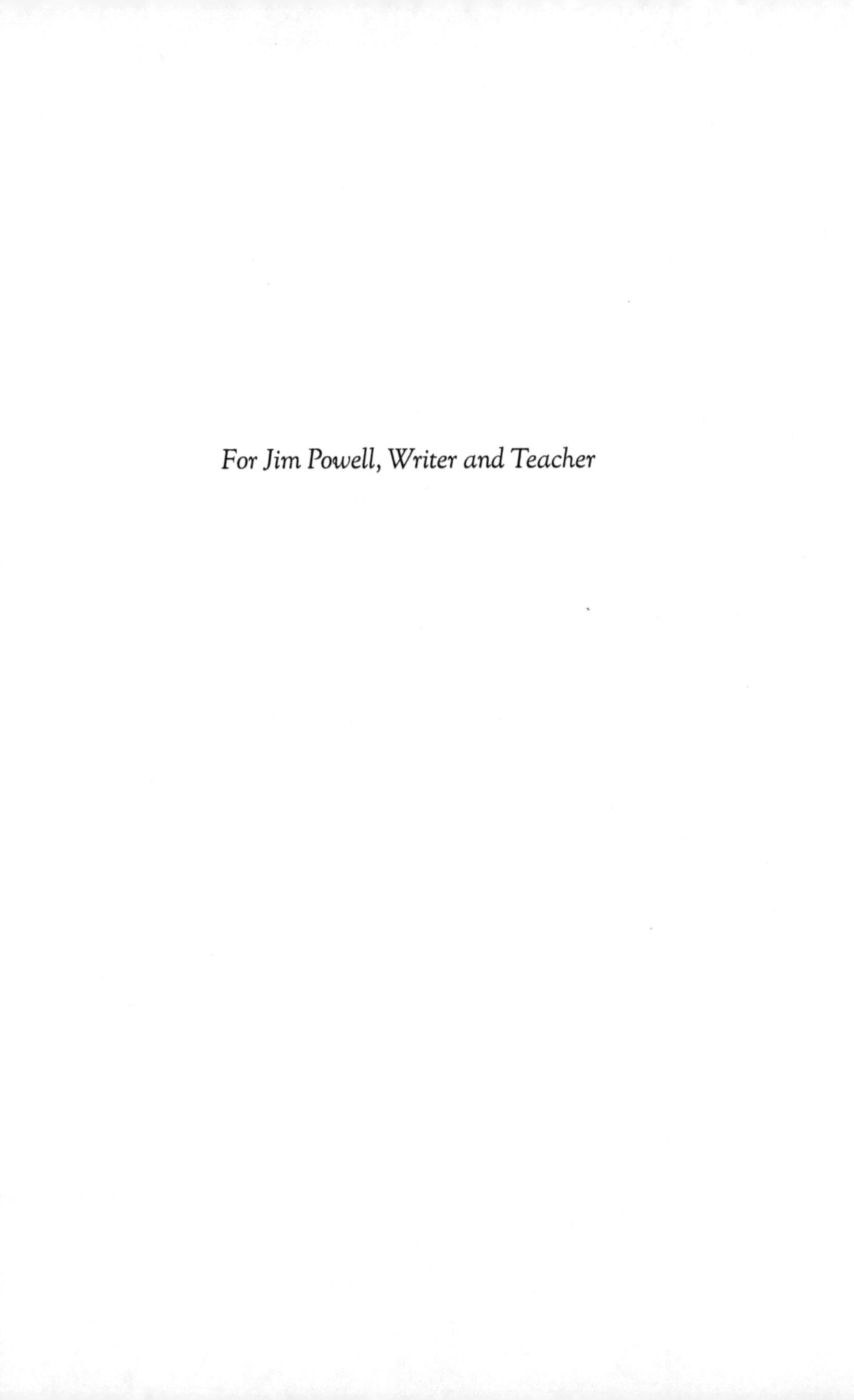

For Jim Powell, Writer and Teacher

Contents

Acknowledgements

"The Quarry" first appeared in *Indiannual 1984*, Writers' Center of Indianapolis, 1984; "Rise Up" first appeared in *Ellery Queen's Mystery Magazine*, August 1998; "God's Instrument" first appeared in *Unholy Orders*, Intrigue Press, 2000; "The Vigil" first appeared in *Ellery Queen's Mystery Magazine*, June 2006; "Forget Me Never" first appeared in *Ellery Queen's Mystery Magazine*, June 2008; "No Mystery" first appeared in *Ellery Queen's Mystery Magazine*, April 2011. The remaining stories are published here for the first time.

Introduction

This volume contains tales I collected during my nearly four decades as a reporter for an Indiana newspaper. Without exception, these are stories which did not appear in the paper, being too offbeat, too paranormal, or simply having too much in them that was unexplained. Or because they were told to me "off the record," a wish I've respected, even after the passage of decades, by changing names and other details. For reasons I don't fully understand, each was a story I had to write, even if no one read the results but me. Eventually, though, I found I had enough of them for a book, which you now hold.

The editor of this volume asked me to jot down some autobiographical notes to flesh out this introduction. She observed that, while I narrate each of the tales, and am in fact a character in most of them, I give very little of my background away. I seldom mention, for example, that I'm married. I told her that a reporter doesn't normally include things like that when writing a story. We don't give our own names—except in the byline—or describe ourselves in detail or even in passing. Still, it occurred to me that, if I declined to use this introduction to describe myself, I might use it to describe my professional specialty and my newspaper and my boss.

The key to success in journalism is the specialty. Young reporters are recruits in an army, learning the basics while they look for their niche, or rather the ladder they'll use to ascend the ranks. For a reporter, the possibilities include politics, consumer affairs, social issues, business, crime, and what my paper called "nut stories." This last category isn't covered in journalism school, but every large paper has at least one nut story specialist, a reporter who covers the sightings of UFOs and ghosts, who interviews the visionaries and doomsters and the people a half step out of sync who see things in the shadows or live in the shadows themselves. Often the assignment requires no writing at all, only patient listening. When nut stories make the paper, they may run as tongue-in-cheek features or semi-serious "unexplainables." In either case, there is a trace of the tabloid about the tales that makes them disrespectable and, in journalese, "soft," a quality they have in common with comics strips and horoscopes and agony columns. The reporter who specializes in nut stories can acquire this softness by association and so lose the aura of the true journalist. All of which means that, as a career ladder, the nut story specialty has very few rungs. But it is the specialty I chose and the reason I have the following tales to tell.

The newspaper that paid me to investigate these stories was the *Indianapolis Star Republic*, born in 1919 when two competing dailies, the *Star Sentinel* and the *Hoosier Republic*, merged. In my opinion, the paper peaked during its first decade, when, shoulder-to-shoulder with another Indy daily, the *Times*, it fought against the Ku Klux Klan's attempt to take over the state. When I hired on in the late seventies, the old timers told second-hand stories of the night of the great Klan march down Meridian Street, when a mob broke out the windows of the *Star Republic*'s Monument Circle offices, and of the special edition that hit the streets an hour later. Eventually, I told third-hand versions of those stories myself.

After those brave days, the paper slid gently downhill. It survived the city's other dailies because it slid more slowly or perhaps because it started from a higher point. But in surviving its rivals it suffered, too. Without the challenge of competition and debate, the *Star Republic* calcified, until its editorial positions became as fixed as its mailing address. This was also due in part to the paper's having been owned by the same family for most of its life. In addition to the owners, there were five or six other "*Star Republic* families" whose members dominated the various staffs. It was rare to find an employee who won a job without some inside aid and not uncommon to meet especially well-connected individuals with ties to multiple dynasties.

Finally, a word about the man brought in to oversee this complacent and unmotivated work force, my boss, E.N. Boxleiter. His bachelor's degree, like mine, was in English, but his graduate work was done at two distinguished schools of journalism, the *Kansas City Star* and the *Chicago Tribune*. He was an exception to the *Star Republic*'s rule of family, as he owed his job only to his ability and his credentials. Boxleiter was the professional who made the train run on time, the gunfighter h ired t o c lean u p t he t own. The expression he wore as he went about this work always suggested that the job would never be finished.

It's difficult for me to picture Boxleiter standing. Because of he was short of stature, standing diminished him, and he spent little time on his feet. His natural position was seated behind his large wooden desk, alone, grimly facing the mass of incompetence assembled on the other side. I was a member of the opposition in his eyes, though set slightly apart by my nut story specialty.

It would be oversimplifying to say that Boxleiter encouraged me in the pursuit of my stories. In the beginning, he adopted the professional's attitude: The assignments he gave me were tawdry nuisances pressed on the paper by a steady stream of crazies and freaks. My only service was clearing his desk of them. Eventually, I came to see this superior stance as a pose, intended to hide an interest very like my own. It's true that he barely finished s ome o f the stories I handed in—usually the stories the paper actually used—but others he pored over as though he was looking for something hidden. It may even be that his secret curiosity fathered my own fascination with these tales.

I hope you'll find the stories in this volume—and any that follow—as fascinating as I have. Perhaps, given your unique experience and perspective, you'll see an answer or a pattern that escaped Boxleiter and his faithful reporter.

RISE UP

It is impossible to know what percentage of Christians go to their graves in the confident hope of the resurrection, but I would guess that the figure is as high here in Indiana as anywhere in the country. But despite that old-fashioned, stubborn faith, it still can shock a Hoosier to hear of dead Methodists and Baptists rising up and moving on. It shocked E.N. Boxleiter, my editor at the *Star Republic*, so thoroughly that he sent me from Indianapolis to rural Putnam County to interview a witness.

"A living witness," Boxleiter told me, "but if you should happen across any dear departed ones, get their stories, too. Ask to see a death certificate."

Putnam is the second county west of Indianapolis, and much of its beautiful, rolling land is still farmed. I drove out on U.S. 40, the old National Road, past motels and filling stations and whole towns made obsolete when Interstate 70 pushed through a few miles to the south. Putnam's county seat is the aptly named Greencastle, but I was bound for Brick Chapel, a dot on the map nine miles north of Greencastle on State Road 231.

My contact's name was Emily Cooper. She was a retired teacher of history and she'd agreed to meet me at the scene of the miracle—or the crime—a cemetery she'd called Windy Hill. There was no sign to identify it, but I spotted Cooper's little Ford just where she'd said I would, five miles west of Brick Chapel on a road called Dog Hollow.

I parked behind her and climbed the hill on which she stood, following the path she'd made in the tall grass. The grass rippled in the wind, making the headstones scattered around the summit look like rocks at high tide.

"Sorry about the mess," Cooper said. "I've been trying to get Mr. McKammon to mow this grass. He's promised me three times he'd see it's done, and look at it. It's long enough now to bale."

I asked if Mr. McKammon was the cemetery's caretaker.

Cooper laughed ruefully. "He's anything but that. Artie McKammon is the county trustee. This is a trustee cemetery, meaning one that's no longer active. At least, it isn't supposed to be active."

She led me down the far side of the hill to a bare patch of earth. It was a very crisp rectangle, approximately six feet by four.

"That's where Clyde Werkman was buried. I'm certain of

it. I come out here once or twice a year to put a flower on my grandparents' plot. They're Grants, up toward the crest of the hill. They were Methodists. Windy Hill used to be the cemetery for a little Methodist church that stood over in that grove of trees."

She pointed to a little vale filled with mature sycamores. There was no sign of a church or even a spot to put one.

"The church burned down in the early fifties and the congregation moved down the road to the church in Brick Chapel," Cooper said. "But Windy Hill Cemetery stayed active for a while, as you'd expect. Widows and widowers wanting to be buried with their spouses, children wanting to be with their parents. None of them knew what would happen to the place, of course. If they could see the grass taking over, they might have opted for cremation.

"By and by, the burials stopped and the church in Brick Chapel decided they couldn't afford to keep up two cemeteries, their own and this one. So Windy Hill went over to the county trustee. When I was little, my parents used to joke about ending up with the trustee, which back then meant ending up on the dole. That was before welfare, you see. I never dreamt the trustee could get you after you were dead."

I asked Cooper about the other disappearances.

"Right," she said, becoming all business again. "I noticed that Clyde was gone because I always stop by his grave. Have since I was little. He was killed in action in Korea, which

I considered very exotic when I was ten. Anyway, when I noticed him gone, I thought, if it weren't for me, who would ever have known? This same thing could be happening at other inactive cemeteries all over the county. All over the state maybe.

"So I went to see Trustee McKammon in Greencastle. Artie told me to call the sheriff. He couldn't be bothered checking his other cemeteries. Too many of them, he said. Every little country church and crossroads town had one, you see.

"I did get Artie to give me a survey of some of the cemeteries right around here. It had been done ten years ago by some students at Depaw University as part of a genealogy project. The survey listed the number of stones in each cemetery and the names on them if they could be read. I used it to do some scouting around."

She extracted a white business envelope from her purse. Her list of disappearances was printed across its face. "Counting Clyde's, I've identified four stolen graves. A Bessie Stumph, who died in 1968 and was buried in another Methodist cemetery near Raccoon Creek. A William Maynard, died in '69 and buried in a farm plot near Fillmore. And Ethel Frost, a Baptist, died in 1973 and taken from Quiet Valley Cemetery near Roachdale."

I asked if all the graves she'd listed had been disturbed as recently as Clyde Werkman's.

"No. There's a trace of a disturbance where Bessie Stumph

should be. The others are just gone. Of course, the weeds and grass fill in awfully quick. Clyde's plot is still fresh because Martin Helms, our sheriff, had a couple of his men dig it up again. They wanted to see if the body was really gone, or if somebody had just stolen the stone. I told him that was crazy. You wouldn't disturb all that earth just to steal a headstone. Martin said he had to be sure. So they dug and dug and came up with nothing. No body, no coffin, no nothing."

I asked if the sheriff had a theory about the disappearances.

"Yes," Cooper said, "but you're not going to believe it. He thinks it's the work of a satanic cult. He's got it on the brain. They had some grave desecrations over in Hendricks County a year or two back connected with a cult. Now every time some kids tip over a headstone, Martin expects the Apocalypse."

Cooper had the look of a person with something else to say. I asked her if she had a theory of her own.

"I do," she said, "and it's a little more scientific than covens and cults." She took a deep breath. "I've been reading a lot lately about alien abductions, where people have been kidnapped by UFOs and studied and then brought back. I asked myself, why would they just study living people? Why wouldn't they open graves, too, like our own archeologists? It makes perfect sense."

Except that the alien scientists had also taken the headstones. I broached the objection.

"I wondered about that, too," Cooper said. "I could only think that they intended to bury the bodies again when they were through with them. Bury them somewhere else, I mean," she added, looking up.

I looked up, too, seeing hazy blue sky but picturing a row of unmatched headstones tucked away in some quiet crater on the moon. Cooper wasn't smiling when I looked back down, so I didn't either.

Sheriff Martin Helms was in his office in the court house in Greencastle, but he wasn't happy to see me. He relaxed visibly when I told him I was looking into grave robbing.

"Thought you might be here about the damn election," Helms said. "I'm sick of thinking about that. Been talking to Emily Cooper, have you? Hearing the latest about the UFO menace?"

I told him I'd heard a little about satanic cults, too.

"Don't go reading that the wrong way," he said. "Take devil worshippers seriously and some people think you take devil worship seriously. They're two different things. Just because an idea's nutty doesn't mean that people won't do mischief in its name. We know for a fact that graves were desecrated in Hendricks County last year by kids with heads full of satanic nonsense. It didn't do any good to tell the relatives of the people whose graves were vandalized that satanism is a joke. The results weren't all that funny.

"I can't say I'm thrilled to have Ms. Cooper laughing at me, this being an election year, but I'll stand my ground on that. When I heard from her about the grave robbings, I naturally thought of those earlier desecrations."

I asked if the Hendricks County cases had involved the theft of bodies.

"Not really. In the worst instance, some bones were taken from an old grave and burned nearby. Mostly it was just vandalism, headstones toppled or broken in two. None of the headstones were flat stolen though. I can't figure that part of our business out. Not that any of it makes much sense."

I asked how the investigation was going.

"It isn't. I haven't got the manpower to stake out every little farmyard cemetery in the county. Hell, I couldn't spare a man to visit each one once a month. We're not even a hundred percent certain that Ms. Cooper is right about the graves being gone. Those lists she's using were put together by college kids for extra credit. For all I know, they made half the names up. It's not like anybody in the trustee's office knows who's in those little plots or gives a damn about them. If the county let the roads go to pot like that, there'd be a revolt."

I reminded him that Cooper had visited Clyde Werkman's grave for years prior to its disappearance.

"Yeah, well, we'll have to take her word for that. There aren't any Werkmans left around here. None of the names

Ms. Cooper gave us have any living relatives that we could trace. That's either a mighty big coincidence, or else those people never existed to begin with."

As I was leaving, Helms thought of a third possibility. "Then again, maybe those space aliens checked the phone book before they beamed the bodies up."

I never got to interview McKammon, the county trustee. His office was on the floor above Helms's, but the path to his door was blocked by his very formidable secretary. She met me at the counter that divided McKammon's reception area in half, asked me my business, and ground her teeth audibly as I told her.

"It's ingratitude," she said when I'd finished. "If it weren't for Mr. McKammon and this office there'd be nobody to care for those orphan cemeteries. But do we ever hear a thank you? Not on your life. It's 'cut the grass' or 'pick up the trash.' And now this. If you want my opinion, this grave robbing business is something somebody dreamed up to discredit poor Mr. McKammon." She leaned forward and dropped her voice. "The sheriff is a Democrat, you know."

A buzzer on her desk sounded, but she ignored it. "There isn't enough money to care for the cemeteries we have already, and more get dumped on us every year." She marched across to a filing cabinet and came back holding a dog-eared folder. "Cemeteries have to report their burials every year, that's Indiana law. Five years go by without a grave being opened and bang, the cemetery is closed forever and lands in our lap."

She pulled a piece of paper from the file and slapped it down on the countertop. "Here are three that are teetering on the brink. One burial a year or less. That'll be three more mouths for us to feed any time now."

I asked her what "closed forever" meant.

"It means no new burials. None. We can't be adding graves to trustee cemeteries. Not with our budget."

The buzzer called out again. "I have to go now," the woman said. "Mr. McKammon will see you sometime when he isn't so busy. After the election, maybe."

I waited until she had locked herself inside the inner office. Then I took the sheet of paper she'd left on the counter and put it in my pocket. I could mail it back later. After the election, maybe.

As the secretary had told me, the list of dying cemeteries contained three names. Two were in imminent danger of becoming McKammon's charges, with only three burials between them in the past five years. The third, Acorn Cemetery, was thriving by comparison. It had had exactly one burial a year for each of the last four years.

The list gave the address of each cemetery. Acorn's address took me south out of Greencastle and then west on U.S. 40 to the town of Manhattan. A few miles south of Manhattan, on a winding country road, I saw a sign for Acorn Cemetery. The sign was made of railroad ties, and its white lettering looked like it had been painted that morning. Geraniums were planted at the sign's base. Not one of the plants held a brown leaf or a dead bloom.

I could smell freshly mown grass as I drove up the gravel drive, and it wasn't my imagination responding to the trim look of the place. A man in a red ball cap was pushing a mower into a shed. I waved to him as I got out of my car and received a serious glare in return.

The cemetery had a beautiful view. It was on a bluff overlooking a field of corn and a bend in a river–the Eel River probably. The graves all faced the river, half a dozen straight rows of them, the grass in between as perfect as a ball diamond's. Many of the graves had flowers planted around them, and two that were close to me were decorated with tiny American flags. I had started to walk toward those two graves when a car door slammed. I turned in time to see the caretaker drive off in a pickup truck without a backward glance at me.

The two patriotic graves belonged to soldiers who had served in the Korean War. One had died in 1953, but the sod over his plot hadn't quite blended in with the grass around it. His name was Clyde Werkman. It only took me a few minutes to find the other names on Emily Cooper's list. Then I paced the rows of headstones for no particular reason, reading names and dates, deciphering relationships, wondering about long lives and short ones.

Before I'd finished, I heard the sound of tires on the gravel drive. It was the pickup truck returning. The caretaker had company now, a stout, gray-haired gentleman in dirty overalls and a petite woman whose strawberry blond hair was shot through with white. Like the stout man, she was dressed informally, her outfit being a housedress and slippers. The man in the overalls took her arm as they climbed the grassy slope to me.

"Hello," the woman called out. "Can we help you?"

None of them looked like he or she particularly wanted to help me. The woman was smiling but frightened. Her overalled escort was just frightened. The other man was angry. Beneath his tan, his face was growing almost as red as his cap.

I told them who I was and that I was following up on a tip about missing graves in Putnam County. I told them that I'd found the graves. I could also have guessed at how they'd come to be in Acorn Cemetery, but I wanted to hear the trio's own explanation.

"We thought that might be it," the woman said. "We never have a stranger stopping. Hardly have anyone ever, except the three of us. When Joe here saw you taking an interest in Mr. Werkman, he came to get Nelson and me. My name is Sally. We're the Acorn Cemetery Preservation Committee.

"We're the ones who moved Mr. Werkman down here from up by Brick Chapel. That is, Joe and Nelson did, but I approved of it. We vote on every addition. It would be wrong to lie to you about it, so we won't. We haven't done anything wrong so far, and we won't start now, not even to protect our secret."

I asked Sally to tell me about it.

"Of course," she said and paused to collect her thoughts. Finally, she chose a beginning that made me smile.

"Once upon a time, this was the cemetery for a tiny place called Acorn. There never was a town really, just a store and the farms around it. The store moved to Manhattan years ago and then closed altogether, but a few of the local families still used the cemetery. The old families. The newer ones used bigger places, some as far away as Greencastle. It's hard to blame them, considering what happens to these little plots once the trustee gets them. They fall into disrepair. Some even get swallowed up by the forest. It's reclaiming a lot of the farmland around here, the forest. And it's getting some of the farmers, too.

"None of that matters to people who don't have family buried in a place like Acorn, people who don't hope to be buried with their loved ones someday. We three do. We're the last of the old families who used Acorn through the years. We're all of us old, and we want to be buried here ourselves. Nelson with his family up there on the highest row, four generations of them. Joe with his wife Ella. And me with my Frank and my mother and her mother.

"That's all we want, but we won't be able to do it if the trustee gets hold of this place. There'll be no new burials then, none, and we'll be parted from our loved ones forever.

So we hit on a plan to keep this place open. We already had our committee formed to mow the grass and decorate the graves. We added the job of moving one grave a year from one of the forgotten cemeteries hereabouts to Acorn. That way we can report a burial a year on the state form and stay open. No one ever comes to check, you see. They don't ask for a name or a death certificate. Just a number."

I asked why they didn't just report a phony burial and save themselves a lot of digging.

My question disappointed Sally. "That would be lying. Besides, keeping this place out of the trustee's hands is only part of the good work we do. The really unselfish part is rescuing poor souls buried in those forgotten places. Your Mr. Werkman, for example, a war hero with no one to remember him. Joe nominated him. You should have seen his grave on Memorial Day; it looked like a parade. We put him next to another Korean veteran, thinking they might have known one another.

"Mostly we try to reunite families. Bessie Stumph, last year's addition, is a cousin of Nelson's, and Ethel Frost was born a Rabb. We're full of Rabbs."

I asked about the fourth name on Emily Cooper's list, William Maynard.

"He was our first addition. Bill was an Acorn boy, born and raised. Married another Rabb, Jean her name was. They were divorced in '59, back when people around here didn't get divorced. The Rabbs blamed Bill and the Maynards did, too, because he drank. They shunned him into moving away. Jean never stopped hoping he'd give up the drink and come back to her. He never did. But we figure they're together now in heaven, so we brought them together here."

Nelson sniffed, and Sally patted his arm. "So you see, we're doing good work and not just helping ourselves. We'd take all the souls scattered around the fields of the county if we could. As it is, we do our best. We'll keep doing it as long as we're able. That is, we will if you'll let us."

I told them I wouldn't interfere. Nelson sniffed again, and Sally took my hand. Joe put his hands in his pockets.

Before I left, I asked them who would plant the flowers and cut the grass at Acorn Cemetery when the three of them were gone.

"That's out of our hands," Sally said. "Maybe some kind person will come along. If not, I suppose the trustee will have us. But he'll have all of us. That's the important thing. We'll all be together."

THE DOUBLE GOER

As I entered his office, E.N. Boxleiter, my editor at the *Star Republic*, threw down the copy he was reading, knocking over a commemorative pen holder. It was his subtle way of telling me he was displeased.

"Do you believe this?" he asked in his most injured tone. "A nice little story lands in our laps. The wire services want it. The television stations are drooling over it. And now some superstitious idiot decides he can take it away from us."

I was familiar with the nice little story. Most of Indianapolis was. The incident had occurred two nights before at Lafayette Square, a big mall on the west side of the city. A man named Carl Schneck had gone to the mall, alone, to buy some undershirts. There he had spotted his five-year-old nephew Billy in the light weeknight crowd. The boy was being dragged along, crying and struggling, by a man

Schneck didn't know. Schneck yelled to the stranger and then chased him when the man ran off, now carrying the boy. Schneck called out for help and soon there was a small posse chasing the man. The abductor finally dropped the boy to make good his escape. Schneck and the others found the child to be unhurt.

Up to that point, it was an interesting story but a local one, unlikely to be picked up by a paper farther away than Fort Wayne. Then an odd thing happened. A woman came out of the crowd. Her name was Enochs. She claimed the boy, thanking everyone and explaining that he had wandered off while she had been paying for a purchase. She didn't know Schneck from Adam, and he didn't know her. He refused to give up his nephew, even after the boy answered to the name Paul and identified the woman as his mother. The crowd that had gathered was understandably confused, but the weight of evidence appeared to be against Schneck and he was persuaded to call his sister to check on his nephew's whereabouts. Billy was safe at home, watching television. Carl Schneck had been responsible for the timely rescue of the wrong little boy.

The story had a lot going for it: action, drama, and a twist at the end that seemed to reveal the hand of fate. A security guard at the mall had passed it on to the *Star Republic*, and we'd released it to central Indiana. Now the wire services wanted more copy and a picture of the two boys, and Mr. Boxleiter was upset.

"This guy Schneck refuses to give us his sister's address or her married name," Boxleiter told me. "He said it would be bad luck or something to get the kids together. I want you to go talk with him. Find out what he's up to."

I asked him whether he wanted a story or just the sister's address.

"A story," Boxleiter said. "We've already traced the sister. The guy's not dealing with amateurs. Her married name is Tippman. I've got a team going to see her this morning, and the Enochs lady is bringing her kid over, so we'll be all set. You find out what's worrying Schneck. We may be able to use it in the follow-up."

Carl Schneck wasn't home at his west-side apartment. One of his neighbors directed me to a factory on Tenth Street where Schneck worked as a welder. I found him in an outbuilding identified by a hand-painted sign as the "Pipe Shop." The inside of the shop was a clutter of hoses and tanks backed by old metal lockers. Schneck looked up when I called his name from the doorway. He was entertaining a small group of men by strapping a tank of compressed gas onto a hand truck. The loungers got me the interview; Schneck didn't want to discuss his business in front of them. He led me into the back of the shop, to an narrow aisle formed by racks of dark blue pipe.

Schneck stood about five foot six. He was older than I'd expected and he looked overweight in his soiled coveralls. An unlikely hero, I thought, and an unhappy one. While

I recounted the incident in the mall, he listened quietly, without denying or adding a thing.

When I congratulated him on the rescue, he waved his hand and said nothing. With no progress made and nothing left to stall with, I asked the big question. Why was he against the boys meeting?

"Publicity," Schneck said. "You know, their names and addresses in the paper. The guy who tried to grab that Enochs kid is still out there. He may decide to try again, or he may go after my nephew Billy."

It was reasonable, but not right somehow. I noticed that Schneck's right hand rapped the wooden pipe rack next to him when he mentioned his nephew. It reminded me of something Boxleiter had said. I asked Schneck if he thought it would be bad luck if the two boys met.

"No," he said, tapping the wooden rack again.

I told him that we could do the story without mentioning the boys' last names. I told him all we were really interested in was a picture of the two of them together.

Schneck looked down at his shoes while I spoke. "Those two boys were never meant to be together," he said.

He looked up, gave me a long stare, and dove in. "You may not think it's strange that I mistook that Paul kid for my nephew. For all you know I'm one of those uncles who only comes around at Christmas. Well, I'm not. Little Billy means a lot to me. I see him every chance I get. I've watched him grow up from a baby. And I thought that kid was Billy. I was sure. It wasn't just the excitement. When that woman came up and claimed him I gave him the hardest look I could. I was sure. That kid didn't resemble Billy. He was Billy. The face, the eyes, the hair. He's Billy's double.

"I thought about it a lot that night and I remembered something that scared me." He stopped to think for a second. "Is this just between you and me?" he asked.

I said it was up to him.

"Then it's just between you and me. Have you ever heard of the Doppleganger?"

I told him I hadn't.

"It was a story my grandmother used to tell me. She was from Germany, came over after the first war. She had a lot of crazy old folk tales she used to scare us with. The Doppleganger was one of them. It means double-goer in German. A Doppleganger is a double. Everybody has one out in the world somewhere. That's what she used to tell us, anyway. Seeing your double is an evil omen. It doesn't always mean death, but it often does. She knew some famous cases that had happened back in Germany, and they always turned out bad. In all the stories she told, the person who saw his double was scared sick. Just think of seeing yourself out on the street, walking toward you, and you'll understand why."

I told him it was just a folk tale.

"That's what I thought," Schneck said. "But a lot of old folk tales are based in the truth. There are a lot of things out there that can't be explained. Have you ever seen a double, a perfect twin for someone you knew? Well, I have. I didn't believe in the Dopplegangers last week. Now I'm not so sure. Anyway, I'm not taking any chances for Billy's sake."

One of Schneck's co-workers came up behind us, whistling loudly so we'd hear him. "Hey Carl, they got a call for you up at the office. From your sister. Some kind of emergency."

Schneck looked back to me before I could lose my guilty wince. "God damn you people," he said as he pushed past me.

I drove back downtown to the office, thinking the whole way of the Doppleganger and of the superstitious fear some remote peoples still feel for mirrors and photographs. As I began the half-block walk from our parking lot to the office, I noticed a man coming down the sidewalk toward me. He was about my height and build, with dark hair and a moustache like mine. For a second or two I felt my heart speed up as I remembered Schneck's picture of a doomed soul meeting his double. The man approaching me wore an expression of concern, caused no doubt by my own. At close range, our resemblance was superficial, but we hurried past one another with furtive sideward looks. I felt an irrational relief when I was safely inside the *Star Republic* building.

Boxleiter met me at the elevator door. "Something went wrong with that story on the kids," he said. "Our people couldn't get into the house. They heard some kind of ruckus going on inside, but nobody would answer the door."

He gave me the Tippmans' address. It took me back out to the west side, to a suburb called Chapel Hill. I never got into the house either. The front door opened as I started up the walk. Carl Schneck came out to meet me. His eyes were red and his hair was oddly disarranged. He pushed his hand through it as he walked toward me, making it worse. I thought for a moment he would take a swing at me, but he stopped a few feet out of range.

"I was too late," he said. "He's gone. Maybe forever."

I asked him whether he meant Billy or Paul.

"Tippman," he said. "My brother-in-law. He's gone off with that Enochs woman. Seems like he met her a few years ago in a bar. Seems like they spent the night together. Seems like he's Paul's father, too."

Schneck pulled at his hair. "They had a big fight, my sister and Tippman. She hasn't stopped crying. Neither has Billy. I don't know what to do."

I didn't have a suggestion, but I had another question. I asked Schneck if he still believed in Dopplegangers and the bad luck they brought.

All he could do for a second was stare at me. Then he made a wild gesture toward the house. "Are you telling me you don't?"

GOD'S INSTRUMENT

Many residents of Indianapolis can tell you where they were on November 19, 1979 when they first heard of the Mitchell Street Disaster, a freight train explosion that killed over twenty people. A few will also remember a macabre detail of the tragedy, the story of a victim who phoned home to say he was all right—after he had died. Ten years later, when I was told to write an anniversary piece on the accident for the *Star Republic*, the mystery of that long distance call was still unsolved.

I could have written a story on the Mitchell Street explosion without leaving the office, using my own memories and the thick file of clippings from special editions of the *Star Republic*. But E.N. Boxleiter, my editor, wanted the human element, a term he considered his own coinage, so I reread the old clippings looking for human elements to interview. I selected a fireman, two survivors, and the father who had received the call from his dead son.

I began with Lieutenant Ward Aikers of the Indianapolis Fire Department. He was one of scores of fireman who had responded after the explosion, and he had been decorated for bravery in the fight against the huge fire touched off by the accident.

"You ever been on a train that derailed?" Aikers asked me. His dark skin was dull under the florescent light in his windowless office and his eyes were tired. I'd caught him at the end of a long shift. "I was once. Years ago. The train was just pulling out of the Union Station in St. Louis. You think of a train derailing as a big thing, like an earthquake or a plane crash, but to me it just felt like a bump. Course, we weren't moving very fast.

"That must have been what it was like the day of the Mitchell Street thing. This long freight was coming into town from the east, just passing through Indy, not stopping at all. The train had slowed way down for all the street crossings out on the east side of town. Barely moving. Then, at the Mitchell Street crossing, a tanker car jumped the track. Just a bump, right? That car dragged along for half a block, spilling more and more gasoline as it twisted, with its wheels throwing up sparks from the roadbed. Then blam! The car went up. It was like a blockbuster bomb had hit square on the tracks.

"Cryer's Lumberyard was right there next to the crossing.

Nobody inside the building had a chance. Six dead. The only survivors were some guys working out back in the open lot. On the other side of the tracks was a packing house, Heineman's. Flattened, practically. Twelve dead."

Aikers sank deeper into his chair. "We fought that fire in the lumberyard and then in the warehouse next to it and then in the factory next to that. When it was over, late the next day, three more were dead. Firemen. Twenty-one killed in all, and a lot more hurt.

"Oh yeah, that," Aikers said when I asked about his medal. "That was mostly for just being on my feet at the end of the fight. Toughest fire I ever worked, Mitchell Street."

He sat for a while looking back, his heavy-lidded eyes slowly closing. By way of wrapping up, I asked him if he remembered the story of the dead man who had called his father.

"I remember three dead fireman," Aikers said. "That's enough." He recited their names for me from memory.

As Lieutenant Aikers had recalled, some of the men working outside in the lumberyard that day had escaped the explosion. I had already gotten the names of those lucky few from the *Star Republic* clippings and compared the list to a current city directory. There had been two matches. Now, I used a pay phone to track the first man, Tommy Lee Taber, to the discount tire store where he worked. I judged from its address that the store wasn't more that a mile from the former site of Cryer's Lumberyard. The store's manager answered my call and went off in search of Taber. I held the line for five minutes and received nothing for my trouble. Taber hung up with emphasis as soon as I mentioned Mitchell Street.

The second survivor, Douglas Hayes, was more cooperative. I called his home and was referred by Mrs. Hayes to a small insurance office that her husband owned and operated. "He'll be very happy to talk with you," Mrs. Hayes predicted.

She was right. "I'm your man," Hayes told me over the phone. "Come on over."

His directions took me to Castleton, a once-quiet area of northeastern Indianapolis now awash in the city's rising tide of shopping centers and office parks. In a modest office building off Shadeland Avenue, I found the Hayes Insurance Agency. Douglas Hayes was a tall, lean man of about thirty with thinning light brown hair and a practiced handshake. He wore a sports coat with a plaid of brown and white and sky blue. The blue was repeated in his tie, which he tugged absentmindedly as he spoke.

"If you're looking for human interest on the Mitchell Street tragedy, I guess I qualify," Hayes said. "That day turned my life around, that's for sure. I've spoken of it often at church functions and motivational seminars. It was the bolt of lightning that knocked me from my horse, you might say.

"I was the original dead-end kid in those days. Born and

raised down in Kentucky, outside Louisville. Sort of raised, that is. Product of a broken home. No father. My mom kicked me out about the same time I dropped out of high school. I had six or seven jobs here and there around southern Indiana before I arrived in Indy and hired on at Cryer's. I worked a forklift out in the yard with a pal of mine, Tom Taber."

I told Hayes of my phone call to Taber and his reaction.

Hayes shook his head. "Tom always was a little short-fused. Drunk when he had the money and mean when he didn't. I was the same way back then. There but for the grace of God, you know what I mean?

"The day of the accident, Tom and I were way in the back of the property, in among some old stacks of lumber. Catching a smoke, to tell you the truth, and trying to stay warm. I can't remember hearing the train. Trains came by the yard so often that you stopped noticing. There was nothing like a warning. The first explosion knocked us down, and we looked up to see a fireball coming right at us. I still see an orange wall of fire against a gray sky some nights in my dreams.

"Tom and I didn't think or look around or plan. We just ran away from that fire. We were only a few steps from the chain link fence that bordered the yard. Ten feet tall that fence was with barbed wire on top, and we went over it like it wasn't there. I could feel the heat from the fire on my back through my coat. That kept me moving.

"You could say that I've been running from that fire ever since," Hayes said. His smooth transition reminded me that I was hearing a well-rehearsed speech. "Seeing friends and coworkers taken like that, in the wink of an eye, it woke me up. I realized that I had been spared by God, that He had more in mind for me than I knew. I finished high school, went into the army, and then worked my way through Earlham College, where I met my Peggy." He turned a framed photograph that stood on his desk around to face me. It showed a smiling woman and two smiling children.

Hayes was smiling an identical smile when I looked backto him. "So you see," he said, "the Mitchell Street Disaster was really the Mitchell Street Miracle for me."

His use of the word "miracle" provided me with a smooth transition of my own. I asked Hayes if he remembered the story of the dead man who had called his father.

Hayes nodded, his smile suddenly gone. "That was another friend of mine, Art Kealing. He'd worked out in the yard with Tom and me until a week or so before the accident. Then he'd been promoted to the office. I'd thought it was a great thing for him, but. . ."

His voice trailed off. When he resumed his story he spoke slowly, searching for each new word. I understood that we had strayed beyond the material he used in motivational seminars.

"Mr. Kealing showed up about an hour after the explosion. He told everybody that he'd heard from Art, that

Art was okay. I thought that Art must have been out running an errand or something when the train came through. I helped Mr. Kealing search the crowd that had gathered to watch the fire. He ended up going to all the hospitals in the city, searching. He was sure he'd find him. He didn't stop looking until they identified Art's body using dental records.

"Art had died in the first blast. No way he made any call. No way."

I asked Hayes if he could explain the call.

"No," he said. "Mr. Kealing may have dreamed it, or maybe. . ."

I waited out his silence.

"God works in mysterious ways," Hayes finally said.

My next stop was the apartment where Mr. and Mrs. James Kealing now lived. It was on the south side of town in a retirement community that called itself a village but was actually a large brick building. The Kealing apartment was on the fourth floor, and I climbed to it on a stairway that rose up one side of the building in its own glass-walled enclosure. I hadn't called ahead for an interview. Judging from the old stories I'd studied, the Kealings hadn't been appreciative of the press at the time of the accident. I had no way of knowing whether their attitude had changed.

It had not. The door of their apartment was opened by Mrs. Kealing. Over the top of her closely clipped gray head I had a brief glimpse of a color television set and the back of the man who sat watching it. When I introduced myself and my business, Mrs. Kealing took a step toward me and shut the apartment door quietly behind her. Without speaking, she took hold of the sleeve of my coat and led me back down the hallway and into the glass stairwell.

When the hallway door had slammed to, she stood with her back against it, facing me. "Not one word," she said. "Not one word do you say to my husband about Arthur." She was a plump woman dressed in a brightly colored exercise suit and athletic shoes. Her angry expression was contradicted by a tiny gold butterfly pasted to one lens of her glasses. "Leave us alone," she said. "Please. I knew you people would be stirring things up again, I just knew it. Ten years. Ten years, and only in the last few months has Jim found peace. If you only knew how haunted Jim had been through all those long years, you'd never bring that awful day into his mind again."

I asked Mrs. Kealing if it was the unexplained phone call that had haunted her husband.

"No," she said scornfully. "Not that. I don't know if I've ever believed in that call. Jim swore by it: a two-second call, 'Dad, I'm okay,' and then nothing but the sound of fire sirens. I've always felt Jim must have imagined it. Or misunderstood someone. He doesn't hear so well.

"No, it wasn't that call that troubled him." She stared at me for a long time. When I didn't disappear, she sighed. "There was bad blood between Jim and Art just before the end. They'd been great pals until Art fell in with a wild crowd after high school. Then he and his dad had some terrible fights. Just arguments, I mean. Except for the last one. Art struck his father that night. They never spoke again."

Mrs. Kealing held her arms crossed against her chest. I could see her breath in the cold air of the stairwell. "That's what bothered Jim so, that Art died without ever saying he was sorry, and, worse, that Jim never had a chance to forgive him. Art would have come around, I know. It was just a stage a boy has to get through. Only Art never had the chance.

"Anyway, like I told you, Jim finally put it behind him a few months ago. I don't know how he did it, but God knows I've prayed and prayed that he would. Now that he's found peace, I won't let anything hurt him again."

Or anybody. I thanked Mrs. Kealing and returned to my car. I left the south side, heading nowhere in particular. I'd found enough of the human element for several stories, but I wasn't satisfied. The mystery of Art Kealing's last phone call was still unsolved. I'd been handed several theories. It had been a dream or a misunderstanding or, perhaps, an act of God. That last idea was the most attractive, but it was undermined by a tiny concrete detail that Mrs. Kealing had tossed my way. Jim Kealing had heard sirens during that call. That placed the caller near the Mitchell Street site.

My tired Chevrolet was way ahead of me. It had found its way onto I-465, the beltway that circles Indianapolis. It's the road to take if you want to end up where you started, which seemed appropriate suddenly. I followed the highway north again to Castleton. It was after business hours, but the front door of the Hayes Insurance Agency was unlocked. The door to Douglas Hayes' inner office stood open. Hayes still sat at the desk where I'd left him, but he'd lost his jacket and tie. In exchange, he'd acquired a bottle of Jim Beam and two glasses. He held one glass out to me as I entered.

"You see," he said. "I knew you'd be back."

That was more than I'd known myself, but I didn't argue with him. Hayes had the look of a man who wanted to talk. I sat down to listen.

"You talked to Tom, I'll bet," Hayes said. "I knew old Tommy Lee couldn't keep his mouth shut. Probably didn't see any reason to. Probably still thinks it's funny, God help him.

"I don't. I knew the second I'd hung up from calling Mr. Kealing that day that I'd done the worst thing I'd ever do in this life. The meanest, most inhuman thing."

The office was dark, except for the area lit by a tiny desk lamp. Hayes sat at the edge of its circle of light. "It was supposed to be a joke, if you can call something that hateful a joke. We knew Art was dead—we were pretty damn sure, anyway—and we weren't too broken up about it. We hated his guts, thought he was a traitor, you know, promoted up to the office and giving us orders. My first idea was just to call his father and give him the news, be the one to stick the knife in him. I must have hated Mr. Kealing, too, just for being around. Then I got a better idea, a really terrible one. It came into my head while the phone was ringing. I pretended to be Art.

"When Mr. Kealing showed up looking for his son, I felt a sick cold run through me. I wandered through the crowd that day more frightened than I'd been after the explosion, certain that if the people around me found out what I'd done, they'd throw me into the fire and cheer it on.

"I went through some bad days after the accident. I was really close to the edge of the pit. Then I got the idea that saved my life." Hayes leaned toward me across the desk. "It came to me that maybe I hadn't been acting for the devil that day. Maybe, after all, I'd been acting for God. Maybe He'd used me to get a message through to Mr. Kealing from his son, the message that Art was all right, that he was safe, wherever he was.

"That thought is what really redeemed me and put me on the right path. Whenever I talk to people now about Mitchell Street—I can't help talking about it—whenever I say that I was spared by God, that's what I'm really thinking inside. That God turned the most hateful thing I ever did into a service, by making me His instrument."

Hayes' words were more confident than his delivery. I understood that he wanted me to confirm his rationalization. Unfortunately, I'd spoken with Mrs. Kealing. I knew that her husband had not been comforted by the long-ago message that his son was "okay."

Hayes seemed to read my thoughts. As I rose to leave, he said, "Mr. Kealing's forgiven me. He really has."

I hesitated, and he plunged on. "I called him a few months ago to confess. This ten-year mark coming up had Mitchell Street on my mind again. I was drunk and all worked up when I called. All I could say was, 'I'm sorry. I'm so sorry for hurting you.' Then Mr. Kealing cut me off. He started saying, 'I forgive you,' over and over. Shouting it almost. I swear he did. It was like he'd been waiting all these years for me to call."

I asked Hayes if he had identified himself.

"No," he said. "I was crying too hard. Couldn't talk. Mr. Kealing was crying, too. After a little while, I just hung up."

I stood there in the doorway of the darkened office for a time, feeling a cold wind through the paneled walls. Then I told Hayes that I thought he was right. He had spoken for Arthur Kealing. I didn't mention that he'd done it nearly ten years after Kealing's death.

I left Hayes crying at his desk and went back to my own to write the story of Ward Aikers and the three dead firemen.

INSIDE LOOKING OUT

I couldn't remember whether I'd read the article about the old farmhouse being moved on the northwest side of Indianapolis. After years of working as a reporter for the *Star Republic*, I'd learned to recognize and pass over the routine stories, the dog-bites-man pieces I'd read many times and probably written once or twice. I'm certain I didn't even glance at the illustration that accompanied the article, the photo that caused all the fuss. It was a color shot of a Gothic Revival house with half its paint gone but its gingerbread trim intact.

The photograph and the initial article appeared in the *Star Republic* on a Tuesday, the day after the hundred-year-old house was moved. The picture reappeared in that Wednesday's edition, next to a completely new story, one I was certain to read on the strength of its headline: "House Photo Raises Supernatural Questions."

It seemed that the Tuesday edition had barely hit the driveways of Indy before people were calling our city desk, claiming they could see a little girl in a blue dress in the uppermost window of the house. That struck these observant subscribers as newsworthy because, at the moment the photograph was taken, the house was traveling north on Lafayette Road, heading for its new home near the intersection of Lafayette and Moore.

Tuesday's article had described the house as "unlived-in for years," but that didn't deter the callers. In fact, it gave them an explanation for the figure in the window, one expressed in the Wednesday piece by Nancy Hyland, a retired bank secretary.

"It's a ghost," she was quoted as saying. "I've stared at that picture until my eyes crossed, and I can see it plain as day. Her hands are on the windowsill and her face is back in the shadows. She's wearing a dress of robin's egg blue."

The article went on to quote the *Star Republic* photographer who had taken the picture, one Randy Tobias. I expected the cold water treatment from him, but I didn't get it. In fact, what Tobias tossed on the fire was closer to gasoline. "I thought I saw a little girl up there at the instant I snapped the shot," he'd said for publication. "But when I looked up from the viewfinder, she was gone."

A representative of the house moving company, perhaps with his firm's insurance premiums in mind, supplied a more objective voice. "There were no children in that house," the spokesman, whose name was West, had said. "None. The house was checked and secured before it was jacked off its foundation. What you're seeing in that photograph is just reflected light sneaking in under the overhang of the roof. The room's walls are blue, so that patch of light that looks like a dress is naturally blue. The so-called face and hands are just holes in an old window screen."

That note of sanity was seconded by one of the house's new owners, an interior decorator named Vivian Avery. She and her dentist husband had rescued the structure when it had been threatened by a new housing development. "We checked out the history of the house thoroughly," she told the *Star Republic*. "There's no record of any hauntings or unusual deaths on the property. The family cemetery belonging to the farm contained no headstone for a little girl." Then, in one sentence, Avery unstruck her blow for reason and provided the author of the story with a great closing: "Of course, if there is the spirit of a little girl in the house, we want her to know she'll always be welcome."

On Thursday morning, I received a summons from my editor at the *Star Republic*, a gentleman named E.N. Boxleiter. He wanted me to interview a couple in connection with the girl in the window. I thought he meant the new owners of the house, the Averys, and I asked him if they'd changed their minds about having a ghost as a tenant.

"Not them," Boxleiter said. "You're to talk to the parents of the ghost. I just got off the phone with them. At least I think it was my phone. I may have answered my Ouija Board by mistake."

I didn't ask Boxleiter why he'd picked me and not the author of Wednesday's follow-up for this plum assignment. He'd identified me years before as the rightful owner of any story that had only one foot planted in reality.

My meeting with the parents of the ghost, Mr. and Mrs. Morris May, was scheduled for noon, which left me an hour to kill. I killed the first ten minutes by hunting down Randy Tobias, photographer to the spirit world. I found him drinking coffee with two of the photo pool's other leading lights. Tobias was a relatively recent hire who had quickly adopted a long-timer's minimalist attitude toward his job. The only things that set him apart from the older chair warmers were his pony tail and goatee and his vague artistic pretensions.

He shrugged when I asked about his fleeting glimpse of a girl in the window of the old house. "So I didn't really see anything up there, so what? It makes a better story this way. Isn't that what we're here for? To make better stories?"

As his fellow coffee drinkers concurred, Tobias added, "Besides, who's it going to hurt?"

Thinking about that question prompted me to track down Vivian Avery by phone at her design studio. She told me she was just leaving to meet her husband and their contractor at the new site of their old house. She invited me to join them there, and I agreed.

Following Mrs. Avery's directions, I took I-65 west to Lafayette Road. Lafayette carried me north past subdivisions that hadn't been there many years before. Those started out modest in the extreme and then got less so and then much less so. Just south of the serious money, I came to Moore Road.

The northeast corner of Lafayette and Moore was a grassy knoll with a grove of old trees, oaks well past middle age but impressive nevertheless. Next to the grove, still balanced on its trailer, was the house.

It should have looked undignified on its perch of rusted I-beams, but somehow the frame structure's dignity was intact. More remarkably, so were its tall brick chimneys and its gimcrackery—the lightning rods with their glass balls and the lacelike trim beneath the eaves. I couldn't tell whether the rest of the ornate woodwork had made the trip safely; there was so much of it the odd piece wouldn't have been missed. All the tall, narrow windows had survived. Their wavy, bubbled glass appeared to have survived for a century.

Two men and a woman were walking about in a staked off area at the very top of the hill. The woman—Vivian Avery, as it turned out—came down to greet me. She was tanned and slender, characteristics shown off by her white, sleeveless blouse and black slacks respectively. She walked gingerly in her dress shoes down the grassy slope.

"I thought for a moment you were another gawker," she

said when she reached level ground. "We've had a steady stream of them since the ghost article ran in your paper."

By way of apologizing for that, I complimented her on the setting she'd chosen for her house.

"Isn't it wonderful? Everyone thinks there surely was a house here at one time, but there never was. This was a cow pasture, which is why the trees were spared. The minute we get the house set on its new foundation, it will look like it's been here for a hundred years."

We were joined at that point by the decorator's husband, who had been identified in the article as a dentist and certainly looked like one in his beige, summery suit and black, wintry shoes. Dr. Philip Avery seemed designed by nature to counterbalance his wife's enthusiasm. His expression darkened steadily as she described her plans for the house.

"We're going to bring it back to its glory days: the slate roof, the pine floors, the plaster moldings, the works. That's why we saved it in the first place. It broke our hearts when we heard through the Historic Landmarks Foundation that the developers who'd bought the house intended to tear it down."

Dr. Avery still looked heartbroken, but he didn't comment. We'd circled the house by then, coming to the front, and I got my first clear view of the attic window where the little girl or something very like one had been photographed. The sun was too high now to light the room beyond the window, which was tucked beneath the sharply-peaked roof. So there was no patch of reflected blue. I could just make out the tears in the window screen that the house mover's spokesman had mentioned.

"Sorry we can't show you the interior," Mrs. Avery was saying. "It isn't safe, with the house still on the trailer. It would take your breath away if we could. The developer who wanted to raze the house never even looked inside to see what he'd bought. Do you believe it? When we came over the first time for a tour, it took us an hour to pry a door open. They'd all been nailed shut for years. The developer was going to bulldoze all that beauty into a hole, sight unseen. We're thrilled that we saved it, especially after what's happened."

Dr. Avery shuffled his feet at this oblique reference to the ghost. Then he looked down angrily at his wingtips as though they had moved on their own.

I reminded Mrs. Avery that her research had failed to uncover any death that might explain the ghost.

"I know," she said. "But just this morning I spoke with a professor of folklore at Indiana University. Do you believe there is such a thing as a professor of folklore?"

Dr. Avery's eloquent shoes didn't believe it, to judge by the little dance they did.

"The woman told me that a haunting doesn't have to be associated with a tragic death. A spirit can chose to return to a place where it's been happy and maybe to an age when it was happy. Our ghost may have died an old woman in a nursing home. She may have chosen to return as a little girl to a house where she'd once known peace and joy. Nothing we do to the house will take away from that peace and joy, I promise."

I looked for more soft-shoe out of the dentist about then. He surprised me by speaking up: "We're only the caretakers for whoever has the house next and whoever has decided to stay on."

He made his pledge to the attic window. We stood looking up at it for a moment. Then the couple's matching cell phones beeped within a few seconds of one another. I hung around long enough to verify that the callers were of this world.

It was time by then to keep the appointment Boxleiter had made for me with the couple who claimed to be the parents of the ghost. I drove back the way I'd come on Lafayette, back to the suburbs' bubbling edge. Mr. and Mrs. Morris May lived in an addition named Pleasant Hills. I found the entrance across the street from a field in which earth movers were crawling about. It had to be the former farm where the Gothic house had once stood. The earth movers were stripping the valuable topsoil, the first step in what was ironically called developing the land.

Pleasant Hills was perfectly flat. I was left to guess about the accuracy of the first word of the neighborhood's name, and the signs weren't promising. The houses were all identical in size and shape: ranch homes so compact they looked like one-story Cape Cods. What little individuality they had came from the color of their vinyl siding and from the landscaping of their hillless lots. The trim of all the ranches taken together—and there were easily fifty—couldn't match the handiwork on one gable of the farmhouse I'd left back on Moore Road. The Mays' house was light blue. Its front yard was bordered by a white picket fence. Vinyl, like the siding, I noted as I climbed from my car.

Morris May opened the front door to me. I knew him before he introduced himself; his name appeared on a plastic tag pinned to his shirt. The tag also displayed the logo of a large Honda dealership whose "super center" I'd glimpsed when I'd exited the interstate earlier that morning. May didn't look old enough to be the father of a ghost. Or of anyone else for that matter. He was short and heavy, and the extra weight he carried gave him a round-faced boyishness that was accentuated by his bowl haircut.

His wife, whom he introduced as Cindy, was also on the heavy side, but she had a good excuse. She was pregnant and well along with the project. Her deep blue eyes were wet, but her handshake was dry and firm.

She apologized for her moist eyes as we sat touching knees in their tiny living room. "I always get a little misty when we talk about Alberta. We were talking about her just now." She handed me a portrait of a little girl. She had her father's round cheeks and her mother's very blue eyes. "She passed away about a year ago," Mrs. May said. "She would have been seven this July."

"Alberta's that girl in the picture you ran in your paper," May said. Whether he'd cut in because he'd noticed that his wife was close to tears again or just because wanted to have his say, I couldn't tell. "She's the girl. We're certain of it."

I told him that not everyone who saw the picture was even certain that the shape in the window was a girl.

"That's 'cause they're not her parents. A parent knows his child's breathing, the sound of her bare feet on the kitchen floor, her shadow. Even if I didn't know about Alberta's tie to that old house, I'd of known that picture was her. I'd of known her if that picture had been taken in Japan."

May's words rushed out, but he didn't seem agitated or even particularly sad. Mrs. May was smiling now herself. She reached out and lightly touched her husband's sleeve.

I asked what connection Alberta had had with the old house.

May answered. "It was the thing I didn't give her. Her piece of beauty. Look at this place. Look at the whole damn neighborhood. No beauty anywhere. A kid needs that as much as she needs food and clothes. I came through with the food and the clothes. I worked my tail off to do it, too. But I didn't give Alberta beauty. I didn't even realize I hadn't given her any till she was gone, till I saw her in the funeral parlor, surrounded by flowers. That was the way she should have lived her whole life: surrounded by flowers. By the time I saw that, it was too late.

"But you were asking about her and the house. See, it used to stand right across Lafayette Road in that field they're stripping. And Cindy here used to take Alberta over there for walks. I didn't; I was too busy working. I didn't even know about it. Cindy told me after I'd recognized Alberta's picture in your paper: how they'd explored the house, the two of them, and found that blue attic room. Blue was Alberta's favorite color."

I wondered if May had always known that or whether his dead daughter's favorite color had been another detail he'd recently picked up. It wasn't the moment to ask. He was patting his wife's very full stomach.

"I won't make that same mistake again," he said. "This one's going to have beauty if I have to work three jobs. Now that Alberta's found her piece of it, I can go on with an easy mind."

May looked at his watch and stood abruptly. "My lunch break is over. Cindy can answer any other questions you have."

I'd been thinking the same thing myself. We sat listening as May backed his pickup down the drive and roared off. I waited a full minute after the noise had died away for Mrs. May to volunteer her version of the story. When she didn't, I asked her why she'd lied to her husband about exploring the old house with Alberta.

Her eyes grew wide. I noted gratefully that they were now as dry as her handshake had been.

"How did you know?" she asked.

I related Mrs. Avery's testimony regarding the doors that had been nailed shut for years.

"I won't say anything that might end up in the paper," Mrs. May said.

I closed my notebook, and she nodded. "We never even went near that old house, Alberta and me, much less went inside it. I never gave the place a thought until Morris saw that story about the ghost picture. It lit him up like I haven't seen him since Alberta died. Morris doesn't have any religion. He didn't have nothing to hang on to when Alberta was taken. Nothing to give him a little hope, even.

"Not until he saw that picture. He kept saying, 'Could it be? Could it be?' He couldn't understand it, since Alberta had died over in Riley Hospital. I told him a ghost sometimes appears where it was happy, not where it died."

It sounded like Vivian Avery wasn't the only one who had spoken to a professor of folklore, but Mrs. May's source turned out to be far better.

"My old grandmother used to tell me that," she said. "But convincing Morris meant explaining how Alberta could ever have been happy in that old house. So I had to make up a story about us taking walks over there and exploring the place. I was glad to do it; it lifted so much weight off

Alberta's daddy. It gave him hope again, and a man's got to have hope if he's going to be a good father."

And a woman needs hope to be a good mother, I thought. I asked Mrs. May if she believed the girl in the window could be her daughter.

"No," she said. "I don't hold with that stuff."

She stuck by her statement for as long as it took us to walk to my car. Then she touched my sleeve lightly, as she had touched her husband's earlier.

"These people who bought the house, are they nice? I know they have all the money in the world, but are they good people? Did they mean what they said in the paper about the spirit being welcome to stay with them?"

I told her I believed the Averys to be completely sincere.

Mrs. May patted my arm again, this time in parting. "Thank you," she said.

NO MYSTERY

That the story of the levitating rocks in Yellowwood State Forest had been reported first by a Bloomington paper, the *Herald*, didn't bother E.N. Boxleiter, my editor. He considered our employer, the *Star Republic*, to be Indiana's newspaper of record. Nothing that happened in the state, not even a gubernatorial election, was really official until the *Star Republic* mentioned it, in Boxleiter's view. Other papers' headlines were only slightly better than anonymous notes.

The headline from the *Herald* was a simple one: "The Yellowwood Mystery." The accompanying story was a little more complex. It described how a man named Gordon Guilford, who was hunting in the Brown County woods, had discovered a large "boulder" high in a chestnut tree. Forty-five feet off the ground, in fact. This had aroused the hunter's curiosity, naturally enough, and he'd returned with friends the next weekend. They'd located the original stone and, while getting slightly lost on the way back to their car, they'd stumbled across a second example, this one in a sycamore tree. Since then, a search of the area by state conservation personnel had turned up three more high-rise rocks, for a total of five.

A Department of Natural Resources spokesman was quoted as estimating the average weight of the stones to be four hundred pounds. He also insisted, a little defensively, that the stones had been placed very recently. Otherwise the forest's civil-service caretakers would have noticed them first.

The article was accompanied by a photograph that clearly showed a large rock high in a tree. The photo's caption, like the story, called the rock a boulder, but it was actually a flat slab wedged into the tree at the point where the trunk split into multiple branches. The slab sat perpendicular to the trunk, giving it the look of a crow's nest on a sailing ship.

Several explanations for the phenomenon were given, ranging from the impossible—that the trees had lifted the rocks as they grew—to the highly unlikely—that the slabs had been blown into the trees by a passing tornado. UFOs were mentioned, if only to be dismissed. The dismissing was done by the Brown County sheriff, who thought the flying stones were more likely the work of "kids mixed with beer." Though why they'd done it and how they'd done it the sheriff couldn't say.

His skepticism was seconded by a professor from Indiana

University, Kevin Karnes, who was described as a "hoax buster" by the *Herald*'s reporter. Karnes scoffed at the idea that the rock placements were supernatural or extraterrestrial. He went on to predict that the hoaxers, whoever they were, would be "caught and soon. The mystery will turn out to be no mystery at all."

Professor Karnes was the man Boxleiter had arranged for me to interview. I gathered that my editor was at least as intrigued by the hoax buster as he was by the Yellowwood mystery. "Get his autograph" was how Boxleiter expressed it.

I visited the IU campus at Bloomington on a mild day in early December. Karnes's office was in the Physical Sciences Building, which was on the same hill as the massive football stadium and built of the same brown concrete. The professor's second-floor office had a poster taped to the back of its open door. It featured a flying saucer with a line drawn through it below three large letter A's. Beneath the saucer was the caption "Alien Abductees Anonymous."

I found Karnes seated at a desk in the comfortable space beyond the open door. He was reviewing some papers while a dark-haired young woman in a wildly oversized sweatshirt stood at his elbow. She looked up at me, smiled, and nudged the reading man. He looked, too, processed the information, and said, "You're the reporter."

When he stood to shake my hand, I was surprised by his height or lack thereof. I'd been deceived by the size of his head, which wouldn't have been out of proportion on a basketball center. His regular features were handsome enough to remind me of Boxleiter's joke about the autograph.

Karnes introduced the woman who now stood a respectful step behind him as his graduate assistant, Gennetta Jones. Jones wasn't given any lines in the scene. I soon learned that, around Karnes, few people were.

"The Yellowwood business is on the Internet already, did you know that? A UFO web site, of course. Encounters close dot com, or something like that. It's listed right after a story on strange cases of dog amnesia in Wisconsin. And there's a link to a site that claims the pyramids were built using a 'lost science' of levitation. I've personally participated in several demonstrations showing how large stone blocks can be moved around using a whole lot of manpower and ropes and pulleys. We conducted one at a limestone quarry over in Bedford last year. Last May, wasn't it, Gennetta?"

The dark-haired woman, whose striking eyes were also very dark, nodded, though Karnes hadn't paused for a reply.

"But people still cling to mumbo jumbo like levitation. They think that, just because a task seems difficult to them, it must be impossible to accomplish without supernatural aid. Now they're talking about levitation in connection with these tree stones. I guess some Egyptian priests wandered into the Yellowwood Forest."

Before we arrived at the forest, I wanted to know how

Karnes had gotten into hoax busting. I was just able to squeeze the question in.

"Via Egypt, coincidentally," he said. "You're about the right age. Do you remember all the pyramid nonsense that was going around back in the seventies? Not just levitation, but how the Egyptians had selected the pyramid shape because if focused mystical energy. How you could sharpen an old razor blade by leaving it in a pyramid overnight. That kind of thing.

"When I was an undergraduate, I had a roommate who accepted all that manure uncritically, just because it was in a book. It showed me how vulnerable people are to cons like that, especially people who aren't trained in the sciences. It's almost as though the human race has a genetic flaw, a fatal weakness for mystery. I've dedicated my life to attacking that weakness head-on."

The woman behind him stirred slightly. She didn't cough or look at her watch, but Karnes got the message.

"Right, Gennetta. We have to go if we're going to visit the forest and get back in time for my two o'clock lecture. But before we head out, take a look at this map."

He pointed to a cork board that hung on one wall of the office. Pinned to it was a large map of Yellowwood Forest with such notable landmarks as Scarce of Fat Ridge and Sour Water Creek prominently identified. Three red pins had been stuck in the map just above Yellowwood Lake. They formed a straight line running due north.

"The red pins show the first three stones they found," Karnes said. "We call them the red line. Just to the east is an incomplete second line, the green line."

He indicated two green pins to the right of the red ones. One was due east of the northernmost pin in the red line. The other was across from the southernmost red pin.

"You can see that the middle pin in the green line is missing. That should be where the rock lifters perform their next feat of prestidigitation, assuming they haven't been scared off by all the publicity. The need to complete a pattern is a common weakness of hoaxers. It's what will trip up these rock people. We'd better head out now. Who's going to drive?"

We decided that I'd follow Karnes's Range Rover in my Chevy, in case I wanted to head straight back to Indianapolis. I said good-bye to Gennetta Jones, who was minding the store, and we set out on the short drive northeast to the forest.

Another advantage of driving two vehicles was the break I got from Karnes's voice. Unfortunately, we still had a hike ahead of us after we'd parked near Yellowwood Lake. It gave the professor plenty of time to tell me about his most recent triumph. He had investigated some crop circles that had appeared in a field of winter wheat near Hopewell. I remembered the case, though I hadn't had a chance to check out the circles myself. I even remembered the solution, but that didn't stop Karnes from describing it proudly.

"It turned out to be the work of the farmers who owned the field, two brothers named Happe. Alonzo and Albert. They'd read about the crop circles in England and decided to fake their own. So they could bilk gullible tourists, probably. It doesn't matter how many of those crop circles are exposed as fakes; people still want to believe in them. Even some so-called scientists. There were a couple of guys from Ball State who were convinced they were detecting electromagnetic abnormalities in the Happes' field.

"Electromagnetic abnormalities," he repeated with disdain. "You can find those anywhere if you look hard enough. They're the scientific equivalent of staring at bowl of pudding so long you think you see the Virgin Mary.

"I came down pretty hard on the Happes. Did my best to humiliate them. To serve notice that their kind of fakery won't be tolerated in my part of Indiana."

If I'd had a map handy, I would have asked Karnes to point out his part of Indiana, perhaps using colored pins. He descended a little from his pedestal without my prodding.

"Not that I really accomplished very much," he said. "The faithful are always ready to stream to the site of any new miracle. Look at this path we're following. It wasn't here the first time I came out. It's been worn since by the curious and the credulous. There's the first rock, about fifty yards dead ahead."

I could just make it out through the leafless trees. At that distance, the brown slab looked like one of the wooden platforms placed in trees for deer hunting, though this would have been an unusually high tree stand. As we drew closer, I saw that it would also have been an unusually thick one. In shape, the flat stone resembled an arrowhead, its two long sides about four feet in length and the shorter base three. It looked to be four to five inches thick. It had been placed so that each side was supported by a healthy branch.

"They matched the stone to the tree with some care, but as you can see, there's no shortage of sandstone rocks lying around. Or of suitable trees, of course."

Getting one of the plentiful rocks into one of the convenient trees had still been an impressive feat. I asked Karnes how he thought it had been done.

"With an old fashioned block and tackle, it wouldn't be as hard as you might think. A hundred years ago, every Hoosier farm boy knew how a block and tackle worked. Now that knowledge is lost, at least as far as the average undergraduate on my campus is concerned. Thanks to television, they know more about tractor beams and magic crystals. A bad education is a kind of slavery."

I flirted with the ranks of the disenfranchised then by saying something admiring about the way the stone lifters had managed to form one perfectly straight line and part of another.

"No great trick," Karnes said dismissively. "Not with GPS, the Global Positioning System. With a hand-held GPS, you could make any pattern you want. The urge to form a pattern is what always trips these bozos up."

He'd said something similar back in his office. I asked him what he meant.

"It's not enough for the average hoaxer to do this stuff randomly. They have to impose a pattern. That tells me that the motive isn't just to baffle people. It's to suggest that there's an underlying intelligence behind these phenomena and, by extension, behind the universe itself. The need to believe in something big is a fixation for these guys. Their anitrational cast of mind makes them the natural prey of a scientist like me.

"And as I said earlier, their pattern, whatever it is, is also the hoaxers' Achilles' heel. It suggests where they'll strike next, like the gap our guys have to fill in the green line."

I asked him if he had the gap under surveillance.

"You'll pardon me if I don't answer that," he said. "I don't want my arrangements to end up in the *Star Republic*."

Karnes offered to show me one of the other rocks, but I'd seen enough. Neither of us said much on the march back to the cars. He was saving his voice for his afternoon lecture, and I was thinking about my next stop.

It turned out to be Hopewell, a small farming town just far enough south of Indianapolis to have been spared the promotion to bedroom community. Something about the way the rock mystery had been more or less laid on Karnes's doorstep made me think the people behind it might have a bone to pick with the professor. That made me think in turn of the Happes, the notorious crop circle forgers. The men Karnes had gone out of his way to humiliate.

I located the Happe farm without too much trouble. I found the brothers in the shadow of a barn, changing a tire on a pickup. They were both big men, both in their sixties, both dressed in heavy boots and overalls and canvas jackets. The one who answered to Alonzo wore a brown ball cap on what appeared to be a hairless head. Albert, who must have been the family fashion plate, sported a hat of red and black plaid. They both looked down at their muddy boots when I mentioned Karnes.

"That guy," Alonzo said. "He said we did the crop circles to cheat people out of money."

"We didn't," Albert clarified.

I asked for their real motive.

They looked at each other and shrugged.

"We read about them," Alonzo said.

"You can't understand something just by reading about it," Albert said.

"You've got to do it yourself," Alonzo said.

Albert gestured toward the old truck. "Take it apart and put it back together."

I pointed out that the Happes had allowed people to think their crop circle experiment was something else.

"That was part of understanding it," Alonzo said, and Albert nodded.

When I asked them if they'd heard about rocks finding their way into trees down in Brown County, the brothers looked at each other again. This time I thought I saw a small smile pass from one weathered face to the other.

"Nope," Alonzo said.

"Why ask us?" Albert added.

I pointed upward to a beam that extended outward from the peak of the barn's roof. Hanging from it was a heavy pulley block and several ropes. It was an example of a block and tackle, the device Karnes had mentioned. This one was used to lift heavy objects into the barn's loft.

"That's nothing," Alonzo said. "Lot of those around."

"No great trick to using one," Albert said. "We could teach somebody in an afternoon."

They shared another smile and returned to the tire project.

"Karnes is probably missing something simple," Alonzo said as I turned to go. "College people are like that."

"Probably something right under his nose," Albert said.

I was so convinced by then that the old men were involved in the Yellowwood mystery I almost warned them not to place the last stone. Instead, I thanked them for their time and went off to interview a likely accomplice.

I obtained the address and phone number of Gordon Guilford, the hunter who had first discovered the rocks, by phoning the Bloomington *Herald*. Guilford lived near Fruitdale, which was about midway between the Happe farm and Yellowwood State Forest. I drove to his house without calling ahead.

I'd realized, perhaps belatedly, that the Happes' plan required that their handiwork in the forest be discovered and reported. Otherwise, Karnes would never have been called in and their elaborate joke would have remained incomplete. The brothers wouldn't have left the discovery to chance, either, as that might have taken years. They would have arranged it.

All of which meant that Gordon Guilford knew more about the business than he'd told the Bloomington paper. At first, it seemed he would tell me even less. When I presented myself at his double-wide trailer, press card in hand, he came very close to shutting the door in my face. That was my impression anyway, based on a guilty widening of his dark brown eyes and a nervous twitch of the hand that held the door. Then he gathered himself and asked me in.

Guilford was a grizzled gentleman only a little taller than Karnes. His trailer's front room was nicely furnished and very neat. There were no hunting trophies on display, no deer heads or hides or gun cabinets. All of the room's personal touches were dedicated to the game of golf or to family. An example of the latter stood on a table next to my chair, a faded color photograph of a woman who might have been Guilford's sister, posed with her husband and two doe-eyed children. I'd never seen the sister before, but she looked quite familiar.

My conversation with Guilford was brief. Without my prompting him, he repeated, almost word for word, the story the *Herald* had reported. I asked him when he'd been hunting, and he named a weekend in late October. I remarked that the leaves must have been beautiful, and he said they had been. I said it was lucky he'd been able to see the rock with the leaves still on the trees. He shrugged. I asked what he'd been hunting, and he said deer, though squirrel would have been a better answer, as he would have had an excuse for looking up into the treetops, a place deer seldom hid. As I stood to go, I asked what gauge of shotgun he preferred, twelve or twenty.

Guilford said twenty, making the mistake many people who don't hunt make about shotguns, the assumption that the larger number means a larger gun. I happened to know that a twenty gauge was a bird gun, something that would barely get a deer's attention.

I didn't ask Guilford about the Happes. My thinking had progressed considerably as a result of my brief stop at the trailer. After saying good-bye to the grizzled man, I pointed the Chevy in the direction of Indiana University.

Kevin Karnes's Range Rover was back in its parking space, but the hoax buster wasn't in his office. Gennetta Jones, graduate assistant, was. She'd discarded her tent-size sweatshirt, revealing a T-shirt that was much more becoming. More interesting, too, since it bore the legend "question authority."

Jones told me that Karnes was still at his lecture. I said I was there to see her. She stared at me. When I'd had my fill of that, I asked her why she was setting stones in trees in Yellowwood Forest.

"How did you find out?" she asked.

I gave her the short answer, which was that I'd recognized her picture in Gordon Guilford's trailer. She was one of the little children in the family photo I'd seen there. I'd realized that after first mistaking the grown woman in the picture for Gennetta. It had actually been Gennetta's mother, at about the same age Gennetta was now.

"I guess I shouldn't have used Uncle Gordie," the assistant said. "I don't want to be in the newspapers. Not yet."

I told her that would depend on her story.

She shrugged. "I did it to get back at Kevin. He used me for sex last summer and then dumped me. Turns out he uses all his assistants for sex. I didn't like it, so I worked up a little puzzle for him."

I asked her why she hadn't just reported Karnes.

"For what? Getting tired of me? This way is better. I'll get my doctorate in the spring. Then I'll give the Yellowwood story to the school paper. The laughing will be so loud, you'll hear it in Indy."

I asked her how she'd managed the thing.

"Putting the rocks in the trees wasn't hard. I had some help. I recruited some of the other women from Kevin's past."

After she'd received a crash course in block-and-tackle theory from the Happe brothers. When I ran that guess by Gennetta, she nodded.

"The Binary Brothers, I call them. I met them during that crop circle thing. They're sweet old guys. Kevin never understood them. He sees the need to be part of something larger as a weakness. Especially if your rational mind tells you the larger something can't be true. People used to call that faith. Kevin feels sorry for people like the Happes. I feel sorrier for him. He doesn't believe there's any mystery in the world. But every person you meet is an incredible mystery. Kevin can't see that.

"He thinks he can solve anything with his instruments and gadgets. He's got infrared cameras out there waiting to record whoever puts the last rock up."

I asked her how she planned to get around them. She smiled at me in a way that told me I'd missed a clue.

I looked at the map with the colored pins and saw what I should have seen much earlier in the day. Stepping over to the map, I traced the red line with my finger. Then I drew a line from the upper green pin to the center red one and from there down to the lower green one. The pattern was already complete. The pins formed Karnes's redundant initial, the letter K.

I asked Jones when the professor would spot that.

"Never," she said. "It would mean admitting that he was

wrong. Besides, it's right under his nose. You never see what's right under your nose."

It was the phrase Albert Happe had used. The farmer had been referring to Karnes's assistant, I now knew. Albert might have thought, as I did, that Karnes was a fool not to have recognized the mystery that was Gennetta Jones.

That wasn't the safest thought for a married man to have, so I wished her luck with her degree and headed north.

SEEING THE ELEPHANT

The channeling craze—the belief that certain gifted individuals can speak for long departed spirits—had been dead itself for more than a decade by the time an Indiana practitioner named Wendell Wagoner came to the attention of the *Star Republic*. Wagoner's claim was phoned in to the newspaper by his doctor, which gave it enough credibility to interest E.N. Boxleiter, my editor. He sent me south from Indianapolis to the town of Greenwood one crisp fall day with some cryptic words of encouragement: "After this, you can add war correspondent to your resume."

Greenwood lay beyond Indy's official border but well within its urban sprawl. Boxleiter's directions took me to a little oasis in the strip-mall maze, a self-contained retirement community called Greenwood Haven. The wooded grounds of the complex contained "independent living" apartments and several gradations of "assisted living," the final one being total nursing home care.

The setup was explained to me by a receptionist named Norita when I asked at the main desk for Wendell Wagoner.

"Mr. Wagoner started out in an independent living unit when he came here five years ago," Norita, a forty-year-old who had to feel like a teenager at the Haven, told me. "Now he's in the Apple Blossom Wing." She dropped her voice to add, "The next stop's heaven."

My visit had been timed to coincide with the rounds of Dr. Sheldon Dodd, physician to about half the residents of the Apple Blossom Wing, including Wendell Wagoner. I found the doctor waiting for me just beyond the wing's automatic doors. He was warming himself before a gas fireplace in a tastefully decorated anteroom, a stocky man with blue eyes as crisp as his suit was rumpled. Those eyes examined me over reading glasses worn well down on his nose, where they made his long face seem even longer. After he shook my hand, he passed his fingers through what remained of his nearly black hair. I wondered if the gesture was habitual and might explain the thinning.

"Trust me, I'm the last person who'd ever believe in the paranormal," Dr. Dodd began, paraphrasing perhaps a hundred other people I'd interviewed over the years. "But I've been seeing Wendell for some time now, since before he was transferred to this wing. I know him and I know his stories. And the persons I spoke to on my last two visits were not Wendell Wagoner.

"I should tell you first that Wendell is suffering from Alzheimer's Syndrome. The common conception of Alzheimer's is that it robs older people of their memories, but it's much more insidious. It really robs a person of his or her identity, which is the sum of the person's memories and experiences, when you stop to think about it."

He stopped so I could think about it. After a suitable pause, I nodded.

"In Wendell's case, the result is particularly tragic. The Wendell Wagoner I knew was a man with some amazing memories, some truly important memories. He was a decorated combat veteran of World War II. He's regaled me many times over the years with stories of the fighting he saw in the South Pacific. Now all that's lost."

Which brought us to what had taken the place of Wagoner's memories. It was a difficult subject for this man of science. He demonstrated that by consulting first the clipboard he carried, then his watch, then the gas fire, and finally his watch again.

"Most Alzheimer's victims eventually become blank slates," he began, choosing his words carefully. "No memories, no identity. Even their faces tend to lose individuality. It's amazing to what degree our expressions, the physical reflections of our thoughts, shape our features.

"In all the other cases of Alzheimer's I've seen, nothing

is ever written on those blank slates again. The single exception has been Wendell Wagoner, whom you'll meet in a moment. As I said, I got to know Wendell when he was a resident of another wing. He was having some hip trouble and needed my help, but he was still sharp mentally.

"Whenever I stopped in to see him, he'd tell me some story of the South Pacific. To the aides and nurses here, he was just an old windbag, one more old man who wouldn't let go of his glory days. He was much more than that to me."

Dodd checked his watch again and set off down a long hallway, gesturing for me to follow. I never quite caught up, so the next part of the doctor's story was delivered over his shoulder.

"I've never been in combat myself, and I've always wondered how I would react. I doubt I'd do as well as Wendell. Few men would. He was an incredibly brave man. Of course, he talked about being scared, but he never really sounded scared." Dodd stopped and fixed me with his glacial stare. "Not when he was himself."

We set off again, weaving our way through parked wheelchairs, some of whose occupants smiled at us or said hello. Dodd ignored them.

"Once the Alzheimer's progressed to a certain point, Wendell began to lose his stories. I'd ask him about specific ones, like the story about the landings at Tarawa, to try to keep them alive in his mind. Eventually, that stopped working.

"Then one day I asked him to describe any battle he could remember. I didn't really expect him to respond, but he started in talking about a massive artillery barrage, bigger than anything he'd described before. And he wasn't talking about battleships doing the firing, which is what our side used in the Pacific Theater. He mentioned something called railroad guns, big artillery pieces mounted on flat cars. Flat cars, in the middle of an ocean. And he described an attack by a hundred or more tanks, and of course that wasn't right either."

We stopped outside a room whose door bore two names, one of them Wendell Wagoner's. Dodd dropped his voice to a near whisper, as Norita the receptionist had done earlier.

"Wendell talked about 'going over the top,' climbing out of trenches to attack across 'no man's land,' and about facing barbed wire and massed machine guns. And he was terrified, which he never had been in any of his other stories. I don't mean he talked about being terrified. I mean he literally shook as he talked. And he cried when he described the bodies strewn across that barbed wire. He'd never cried before.

"I asked him where this had all happened. He said, 'St. Mihiel.' I'd never heard of an island by that name, so I looked it up. It's not an island. It's a place in France. The American army fought a big battle there. *In 1918.*"

The italics were the doctor's own, added by his voice,

which had risen to its original level and beyond. He gathered himself a little and continued.

"The next time I came to see Wendell, I asked him again to describe any battle he could remember. He told me about a fight I recognized from my study of the Civil War, a battle I'm hoping he'll describe for you today. Shiloh."

With that, the doctor pushed open the door and entered the room. He hadn't knocked, but neither of the room's two occupants objected. One lay in bed, his eyes hidden by blue lids and his breathing deep. The other sat up in a wheelchair with his eyes wide open, but he seemed no more aware of us than the sleeper.

Dodd sat down on the bed next to the wheelchair, put his arm around the seated man's shoulders, and addressed the man's left ear. "Wendell, this is a friend of mine. He'd like to hear the story you told me yesterday. Do you remember that story, Wendell?"

Wagoner's only reply was a blink. The whites of his empty gray eyes were remarkably white, or seemed so against the yellow, waxy skin of his face. That skin was dragged down by bags beneath his eyes and by dewlaps at the jaw line. At his temples, the yellow skin was marked by very thin, very dark blue veins that looked like satellite photos of nearly dry rivers. Above them was a full head of white hair carefully combed by one of the Haven's staff, perhaps in the very style Wagoner had once used.

Dodd produced a tiny tape recorder from the pocket of

his suit coat. He switched it on and balanced it on one arm of the wheelchair while he cooed on in Wagoner's ear about yesterday's visit and the story the old veteran had told. From time to time, the doctor looked up at me and smiled nervously, like a man whose dog refused to roll over for company.

"You remember, Wendell. Sure you do. You told me you were sitting around campfires finishing your breakfast, you and the guys in your company. A friend of yours named Jeremiah was cleaning his gun. You heard some firing off in the distance and thought it was a cavalry raid. Then what happened?"

"Cannonballs came rolling through the camp," Wagoner said in an inflectionless baritone.

Dodd glanced up long enough to nod at me. "Cannonballs? On the ground?"

"Rolling on the ground," Wagoner said. "Almost spent. Jeremiah picked one up. It was still warm to the touch."

Wagoner's voice, which had started out as spent as the playful cannonballs, was gathering force. And his vacant eyes were focusing, but not on anything in the room.

"All at once, the drummer boy started playing the long roll. We formed up and marched out. Marched to the sound of the guns."

"What's your outfit, soldier?" Dodd demanded.

"The 44th Indiana Volunteers, Company C," Wagoner answered, a little trace of panic in the words. "We lined up between the 31st Indiana and the 17th Kentucky. Our line was along a little sunken road. We only just had time to get set and they came at us, yelling and firing. We cut them down, but they came again and again and again."

The shaking that Dodd had noticed during Wagoner's retelling of the battle of St. Mihiel was starting again, first in the old man's gnarled hands, then in his arms, then in his shoulders. The doctor reached over to steady the tape recorder.

"At two we fell back and formed up in a peach orchard. The bullets were so thick overhead they cut those trees to pieces. The petals fell down on us like snow. Oh, Momma. Momma!"

The sleeper on the bed behind me was stirring. Dodd tightened his grip on Wagoner's shoulders. "You're out of the peach orchard now," the doctor said soothingly. "What's happening now?"

Following the doctor's lead, Wagoner shifted to the present tense, his eyes wild with fear. "We're falling back. Firing and falling back. The river's behind us. Once we reach the river, we're done. They'll push us right in. I can't even swim. Help me, Momma! Help me, somebody!"

For the first time, Wagoner seemed to notice me. But I was no more help to him than the doctor. Instead of trying to calm the sweating, shaking man with the wild eyes, I asked him his name.

"My name?" he repeated, and I saw that I had helped him

in spite of my curiosity. The shaking stopped, and his eyes lost their strange light. He managed to say, "I don't know my name," and then he slumped again in his chair, oblivious to us and the room.

Dodd checked the old man's pulse and then led me out into the hallway.

"They never were pushed back into the river," he whispered, ignoring the censuring glance of a passing nurse. "They were saved by darkness and the Federal artillery. That night, fresh Federal troops arrived. They counterattacked the next morning and drove the Confederates from the field."

I was tempted to check the doctor's pulse. He was that carried away.

"What we just listened to was an eyewitness account of Shiloh, a battle fought in 1862. Somehow, Wendell Wagoner has become a receiver for other brave men like himself, warrior spirits who are telling their stories through him."

To calm my own heart rate, I stated slowly and clearly a far more likely explanation: Wagoner was simply recalling something he'd read.

Dodd shook his head. "He never read about war. He made a point of telling me that more than once. He was especially impatient with Civil War buffs like me. He couldn't understand making a hobby out of something that horrible.

"Besides, if he was just parroting back something he'd read, why did it frighten him that way? That terror is what convinced me I wasn't listening to Wendell Wagoner. Wendell never showed a trace of that fear, not in any of his stories of the South Pacific. This Shiloh witness and the one from St. Mihiel were both terrified. I'm not judging them, mind you. I'm sure they both did their duty. I'm just saying they can't be Wendell Wagoner."

As he walked me out, Dodd became philosophical. "We demand tremendous sacrifices of our soldiers. We expect them to sacrifice their lives, of course, or the use of their limbs or their sight. Some of them sacrifice their minds. Even those who come through a war in one piece, like Wendell, are affected by the experience for the rest of their lives.

"But this is different," he said when we were once again in the entryway before the artificial fire. "This seems to me to be above and beyond any sacrifice I've ever heard of."

I asked the doctor if he was saying that Wagoner's Alzheimer's was a result of his war service.

"Of course I'm not. I'm saying that Wendell's war experiences shaped him in a certain way. Made him receptive to reverberations of other men who sacrificed so much for this country. Attuned him to them, so that now, when his own personality is gone, theirs are coming through.

"This is Wendell's last service to us, and it's a horrific one. In the final days of his life, when he's earned a little peace if any man has, he's condemned to fight our nation's battles over and over again."

• • •

I drove back to Indianapolis and stopped at the State Library to look up the 44th Indiana Volunteers and Shiloh. I found a brief account of the battle first, and it supported Wagoner's version of events. Then I located a regimental history of the 44th and learned that the outfit had been formed in Allen County, near Fort Wayne. It had numbered just under four hundred men at the start of Shiloh. Of those, over two hundred had been killed or wounded. An appendix contained the names of the men who had responded to the original muster in 1861. Two Jeremiahs were listed, including one in the company Wagoner had mentioned, Company C. He could have been the man who'd picked up the still warm cannonball.

When I asked for more information on the regiment's enlisted men, a helpful librarian sent me across the street to the Indiana Historical Society's new Frank Lloyd Wright revival building. There I was directed to an archive on the second floor. Before I was allowed to enter this sanctum, a guard in a royal blue blazer asked for my driver's license and typed its information into a computer terminal. Then he confiscated my cell phone and my topcoat.

"Can't have any of our valuable papers walking out of here," he said as he took my coat. "No handbags, coats, or briefcases beyond this point."

He had twitchy eyebrows that were so thin I suspected that he'd had them professionally shaped. His last official act was to present a guest register bound in leather the exact same color as his blazer.

"Please sign in."

As I did, I asked him why the society maintained both computer records and an old-fashioned guest book.

"This register," he said, closing the volume and caressing the leather, "will be part of our collection someday. When you sign in here, you do more than enter the archives. You become part of them. You enter history."

That last phrase was running through my head when I arrived in the archive's well lit and largely deserted reading room. There a friendly young woman named Meg, whose brows were unplucked, listened to the third or fourth rendition of my request regarding the rank and file of the 44th Indiana.

"We may have just the thing for you," she said. "Letters written by members of the 44th who served at Shiloh. Really amazing stuff."

She left me briefly and returned carrying an ordinary cardboard file box. I had the lid off before she could get away. The box was full of letters, no two of them on paper of the same size or color.

"Think of these being written by men who witnessed the Civil War firsthand," Meg said with a sigh that told me she'd found the right career.

I thought of telling her that I'd just spoken with a man who'd witnessed the Civil War firsthand. Instead, I asked her how the society had been able to collect letters that had been mailed one hundred and forty years before to farms scattered all over Allen County.

"Oh, these aren't letters written during the war. These were written for regimental reunions. The 44th held a reunion every year until the men were all dead or too old to come. The men who couldn't attend would often write letters to be read aloud at the banquet. That's what these are."

I would have figured that out for myself if I'd just plunged into the letters, many of which began with greetings to old comrades and an explanation of the writer's absence. Included with the letters were reunion programs, the earliest one from 1887 and last, remarkably, from 1938, by which time the attendees were the children and grandchildren of the veterans.

The battles recounted in the letters included Stones River, Chickamauga, and Missionary Ridge. I ignored those and concentrated on Shiloh, forgetting Meg and the room around me, forgetting my original fascination with the variations in paper and handwriting and spelling. All the details mentioned by Wagoner were there, except one. I found the original stand at the sunken road, the later one at the peach orchard, where the flower petals fell like snow, and the last desperate stand at the river, with massed Federal artillery lighting the dusk. I found everything except the striking detail that had begun Wagoner's account: the nearly spent cannonballs rolling through the peaceful camp.

And then I found that, too. It was included in a letter written on tiny sheets of paper torn from a pad. The letter, written in pencil in a clear round hand, had been composed in 1892, the thirtieth anniversary of the battle.

"We were having breakfast, Jeremiah and I. And some of that good old mule kick coffee. Jeremiah was cleaning his rifle as he ate and joking about using the coffee on the barrel. He was quite the one for a joke. We heard the sound of distant gunfire and thought it must be a cavalry raid. We were mad that we were too far away to see the fun. Then something came rolling through the camp. A cannonball! Jeremiah picked it up. It was still warm! He said, 'Hope I'm this warm come sundown.'

"Then the drummer boy began to beat the long roll. . ."

In addition to the cannonball motif, the letter contained something else I remembered from Wagoner's performance: genuine fear. Even though thirty years had passed for the writer, he vividly conveyed how frightened he'd been during the fighting.

I turned to the last sheet and read the signature. Frank de Haas. Now I had the name of the warrior spirit who was using Wendell Wagoner to tell his story. Or I had something else, something almost as interesting.

I carefully repacked the file box and returned it to Meg. Once she was satisfied that I'd been suitably moved by the contents, she asked if there was anything else I needed. I requested the registers that visitors to the archive had to sign to gain admission, the blue-bound books that then became part of the society's collection.

They were right there in the reading room, a whole shelf of them, looking like a stand of yearbooks from a particularly regimented high school. I started with the volume from five years earlier and searched backward, scanning the handwritten names for Wendell Wagoner, the man who hated to read about war and especially disparaged the hobbyist's approach to the Civil War. I'd gone back an additional two years before I came across his signature for the first time. I found the records of five more visits he'd made to the reading room before I gave up my search and left Meg alone with the dust mites.

Once outside I started to call Dr. Dodd with the bad news but decided that job could wait. Instead, I called Greenwood Haven, hoping that chatty Norita was still at the reception desk. She was. I asked her to direct me to someone who could give me the name of Wendell Wagoner's next of kin. Norita could do that herself, as it turned out, using her handy computer. The relative's name was Andrew Gott, and he was Wagoner's nephew.

It took me three calls to reach Gott, an independent painting contractor who was working on a house in the Meridian-Kessler neighborhood, just north of downtown. When I mentioned his uncle, I thought I heard an answering snort, but the cellular connection was shaky. Before we lost it completely, Gott told me I was welcome to stop by his job site.

I found him on the front porch of a brown-brick two-story whose architect had made ample use of ornately carved limestone, including a keystone over the entryway arch that bore the profile of a crouching cat.

"Don't know what the original owners were thinking of with that," Gott said, following my gaze. "Maybe wanted to warn off the mice. You the reporter?"

I told him I was and went on to explain my interest in his uncle. That is, I started to. When I quoted Dr. Dodd regarding Wagoner's outstanding war record, Gott interrupted with a snort I couldn't blame on cell phone static.

"War hero my ass," he said. He was a tall, spare man in his thirties whose perfect pompadour seemed more suited to a desk jockey than a house painter. His skin, on the other hand, was as wind and sunburned as any farmer's. "John Wayne saw as much real combat as my Uncle Wendell did."

I mentioned the landings on Tarawa, Dr. Dodd's favorite story.

"Uncle Wendell never landed on Tarawa, never was on Tarawa, never even saw Tarawa. His unit was stationed on Saipan, but they didn't get there until the island was secure. He spent the war playing baseball and watching B-29s takeoff and land. All his big war stories were hot air.

"Don't blame yourself for being taken in," Gott advised me as he turned his attention back to the door he was painting a bright red. "Uncle Wendell had me fooled for twenty years. I grew up on his stories, knew them all by heart. He was a kind of hero to me, tell you the truth.

"Then my mother died. She was Wendell's sister. And my father, Wendell's brother-in-law, told me the truth about the great war hero. Guess Dad had been busting to tell me for years, but Mom wouldn't let him. It was all I could do to keep Dad from telling Wendell off at Mom's viewing."

Without turning his attention from the brass work he was painting around, Gott asked, "Just what's your interest in Uncle Wendell and his tall tales? You doing a piece on forgotten veterans?"

I related Dr. Dodd's belief that Wagoner was channeling the spirits of dead warriors. About the time I transitioned from St. Mihiel to Shiloh, Gott stood and turned to face me.

"Damn," he said. Then he noticed some crimson drops falling from his brush onto the porch's flags. "Damn," he said again.

While he wiped the stones, I gave him a brief recounting of my time at the Indiana Historical Society and my discovery of Wagoner's many visits. I asked the nephew if his uncle had been interested in the Civil War and World War I, contrary to Dr. Dodd's claims. The painter sided with the physician.

"There was only one war as far as Uncle Wendell was

concerned. His war. I don't remember him mentioning another."

I asked him why he thought his uncle had done all the research and why he had kept it a secret.

Gott gave the porch stones a final wipe and stood again, a smile of understanding on his face. "He had to keep quiet about his research if he wanted to protect his big secret, which was that he'd never seen a battle himself. Don't you see? He wasn't studying those wars. He was studying how men reacted to fighting, what war was really like, something he couldn't know for himself.

"The soldiers in the Civil War called battle experience 'seeing the elephant.' I picked that up from the Ken Burns series they ran on public television. 'Seeing the elephant' is just the perfect way of saying it. For those old farmboys, an elephant was something rare and wonderful, something they'd all heard about but most had never seen. And no descriptions or drawings really do an elephant justice. You have to see one to really believe it. They thought a battle was like that, something you had to experience firsthand to understand.

"Uncle Wendell never had the experience, so he never knew what it felt like. Guess he was desperate to know. Now that I think back, that was what was always missing from his phony stories. The real emotion."

I pictured Wagoner shaking and crying and told Gott that real emotion was no longer missing from the old man's tales.

"Poor guy. I'll go by and see him. Still, he brought it on himself. Guess you've got to be careful where you spend your fantasy time. Once your mind starts to go, you may end up stuck there. Like Uncle Wendell, stuck fighting all those battles he always wanted to be in.

"My mom, if she'd been spared long enough to make it to a nursing home, might have spent her last days dreaming of Jesus and his angels. I'll probably spend mine on some beach with Brooke Shields.

"How about you, buddy?" he asked as he turned back to his work. "Where are you going to spend your twilight time? Something to think about."

THE QUARRY

Ralph Stillwell was a confessed murderer with a unique relationship to his victim. He also had a problem getting anyone in his hometown of Indianapolis to take him seriously. He called the *Star Republic* one day to complain about the performance of the city's police and to see if we would help him confess his crime. We'd provided this service for others in the past, so E.N. Boxleiter, my editor, agreed to an interview. Boxleiter thought the business so important that he pulled me off a story about a Plainfield woman who'd dreamt for fifteen nights running that she was Eleanor Roosevelt.

I started by calling a contact I had in the Indianapolis Police Department. He went off to look for the report of the investigating officers and came back on the line laughing. Ralph Stillwell was eighty-two years old. He wanted to clear his conscience of a crime he'd committed in 1916. In the opinion of the officers, the incident described by Mr. Stillwell had really been an unfortunate accident. They recommended no further action.

My contact's last comment was intentionally enticing: "The police force isn't interested in ghosts."

Mr. Stillwell lived on the near south side of the city, not far from Garfield Park. His house was a neat, white frame with a tiny, manicured lawn. The inside was also neat, but there was something of the acrid smell of a nursing home in the air. Stillwell received me in the parlor. He was a thin man with thick white hair and deep lines in his face. The lines helped create the illusion that his narrow head was being squeezed by his large ears. A housekeeper made noise in the kitchen while we spoke.

"I didn't mean to be hard on the police," Stillwell began. "They were none of them even born when I murdered Otis. They think it's ancient history. Well, it isn't for me. I can't help thinking of it these days. I've lived with it all these years, but now it seems to be taking me over. I guess it may be because my own time is about up. I have a cancer, you see."

I waited without replying. We both listened to pots banging in the next room for a moment. Stillwell made an effort to straighten himself in his chair, but he looked down at a spot on the floor as he began again.

"It was just this time of year when it happened and just this hot. Maybe it's the heat that's got me thinking back. We had a swimming hole then, a bunch of us boys from the southwest side of town. It was an old stone quarry, old in 1916 even. We called it McQuade's, but I can't remember where we got the name. It was all closed up, of course, because it was flooded. They'd hit an underground stream with their digging and their pumps couldn't handle it. The pit flooded so fast that all their equipment was trapped at the bottom, including a narrow gauge railroad locomotive.

"We would have swum there anyway, but that locomotive made the place special for us. Mysterious or haunted or something. That engine became the basis for our challenge, our test of manhood, which is what started all the trouble.

"The water in the quarry was very clean and you could see a long way down, but you couldn't see the engine. The highest point of the edge was an outcropping of the rock thirty feet above the water. Standing on that ledge on a bright summer day, you could see the shadow of something, but you couldn't exactly make it out. Our dare was pretty simple: dive from the topmost edge of the quarry and find the old engine.

"There were seven of us. None of us had made a dive from that height before. One by one over the course of a couple of days, five of the boys worked up their nerve and did it. The engine was about thirty feet down. At twenty feet you could just see it clear and that was about as deep as any of the boys got. As each boy came up from his dive, he described what he'd seen. Every description was spookier than the last. It seems like the engine must have exploded when the cold water hit the boiler. It was all cockeyed and smashed. An awful thing now and not a engine at all, the way they told it.

"Finally, there were just two of us left to make the dive, me and Otis Jayne. Otis was my best friend in the gang, but he was also the runt of the group. He was scared of the thirty-foot dive and the thing at the bottom, too. He had too much imagination; that was his problem. I'd never seen anyone so scared in my life. I wanted to help him and the only way I could think to do it was to promise I wouldn't dive either. That way there'd be two of us to take the abuse of the rest. I'll never forget Otis's face when I made that promise.

"I really meant to stand by Otis. I underestimated the pressure from the others. If I'd been a year or two older, a man you see, I might have been able to take it. But boys know how to hurt a boy. It got so I began to doubt myself. I couldn't tell if I'd really backed down for Otis or if I was just scared. Once I started to doubt myself, poor Otis was doomed. I had to make that dive.

"The worst part was, I didn't tell him beforehand. I went down to the quarry with the gang and Otis came, too. He didn't want me to face the rest of them alone, you see. Anyway, when we got there I walked right to the edge at the highest point and took off my clothes. I never even looked around at Otis. I just squared up to the edge and dove. It was the only way to do it.

"I made a clean job of it, but the force of the water still felt like a smack on the head. I shot down into the dark green like an arrow. When I opened my eyes, there was the engine below me. The water was terribly cold and the cold seemed to be coming right up at me from that black thing.

"I still had momentum, but the pressure of the water was pressing my eyes like two thumbs and making my head squeak. I turned around and swam back up.

"I broke the surface to the sound of five guys cheering me from the rocks around me. I looked for the sixth, but I couldn't find Otis until he called my name. He was standing on the top of the rock face.

"'I'm going to bring you a piece of that thing,' he screamed at me.

"I tried to tell him not to dive, but the other boys were yelling for him to jump and the sound of them filled the quarry. I pulled myself onto the rocks and started to climb. The higher I got, the louder the sound of 'Jump! Jump! Jump!' seemed to get. I'd almost made it to the top when the yelling stopped. I turned in time to see Otis hit the water. It wasn't a clean dive and that scared me even more. I waited for a full minute for his head to break the surface. By that time the other boys were scared, too. They were getting into the water to look for him. I waved them out of the way and dove.

"I made a cleaner dive than the first time, but my lungs were shallow from climbing and running. I needed air as soon as I opened my eyes. I knew in that instant I wouldn't reach the wreck. I'd taken two or three strokes downward when I saw something coming up toward me. It was a big bubble of air, flattened and wiggling under the pressure.

"That bubble was the only thing I saw besides the wreck itself. I never reached the thing, never really got close. I was so spent when I got back to the daylight, two of the boys had to pull me to the bank. We waited for a while and then went for help."

Listening to Stillwell's story, I'd forgotten all about the housekeeper. Her voice now startled me.

"Time we were getting to the hospital," she said.

"Treatment day," Stillwell told me. "I'll have to excuse myself." He looked me in the eye for the first time. "Will you print my story?" he asked.

I told him I'd write it and pass it on to my editor. He seemed content with that.

I might have gone ahead and written the story, but I got the odd idea of visiting the scene of the crime. I cut across to Kentucky Avenue on Raymond Street and headed southwest. A couple of miles later, I saw a sign I must have passed a thousand times without noticing. It advertised the Lake Lee-Ann Fishing Club.

I followed a gravel drive to a small wooden building adorned with a faded metal sign shaped like a huge bottle cap. A counter was set in an open window. It was adorned by the hairy arms of a man in a black T-shirt. Beyond the shack was a small lake. On its far side, a limestone outcropping rose to about thirty feet. Bushes and weeds and even a small tree grew from the cracks in the exposed rock face. I'd found McQuade's.

The man in the T-shirt had a wary look. He'd already determined from my jacket and tie that I wasn't there to fish. To make friends, I paid a dollar for a soda and, while I had my wallet out, I showed him my press card. He shook my hand then and offered his name: Reilly. He confirmed that his lake had once been a quarry, but he'd never heard the name McQuade. The lake's current name, Lee-Ann, had been his mother's, hyphen and all. When I asked Reilly about the lost locomotive, he laughed.

"That story's going to outlast me, I can see that. I first heard it in '63 when my old man bought the place, and people still ask me about it. Who sent you?"

I told him I'd spoken with a man who had seen the engine years before.

"He's pulling your leg," Reilly said. "There's no engine in there and there never was. I have the Indianapolis Skin Diving Club here three or four times a year for practice dives. They've been all over the bottom of that lake. All they found was a flat car, or the frame and wheels from one. The thing's no bigger than your Chevy."

I thanked Reilly and went back to tell Boxleiter that Ralph Stillwell was a fake. Though I was no grizzled veteran, I'd been fed my share of tall tales and I could usually spot them, so it bothered me that Stillwell had taken me in. I chalked it up to the fact that he was the oldest liar I'd ever met.

A week later I opened the *Star Republic* to read the obituaries. I started in the business by writing them, and I still read them first from force of habit. That morning I found the last name I expected to see after my own: Otis Jayne. Otis had died in St. Francis Hospital the night before at the age of eighty-two. He'd worked all his life for one of our meat packing companies. He left no family. I looked Otis up in a city directory. His address was familiar to me. It was the house where I'd interviewed his murderer.

I could call my next move a hunch, but it was really just a lucky guess. Indiana University had started an obituary index for the *Star Republic* back in the sixties. I found a copy and looked up Ralph Stillwell. We'd run his obituary on January 11, 1976. I walked downstairs and pulled the issue. Stillwell had lived in Carmel, a fashionable area north of the city. He'd owned his own business and belonged to every service organization but the Knights of Columbus. I briefly considered trying to contact one of the children mentioned as survivors and then decided against it.

Otis Jayne's housekeeper and I were the whole crowd at his funeral. I stood in the back of the small funeral parlor and tried to untangle the knot Otis had tied for me. I decided that his story was true up to a point. Otis had been betrayed by Ralph Stillwell in 1916, in the last few minutes of his boyhood. Otis might even have climbed to the top of that tiny cliff to redeem himself, as he had in the story. But he never dove. His vivid memory of that dead engine was a lie built of every fantastic detail that every boy who had made the dive and seen nothing had fabricated as a consolation.

I went to see Otis off because I'd failed to dive once or twice in my life and gotten away with it. I felt I understood what had really died that day at the quarry, and why Otis had still mourned for it after sixty years.

UNDELIVERED

"What are the odds of that happening?"

The man with the rhetorical question was named E.N. Boxleiter. He was my editor at the *Star Republic*, the most prestigious daily newspaper in Indianapolis, Indiana. Also the only one. We were seated in Boxleiter's office, one of us comfortably. That afternoon had seen the ceremonial wrenching open of the office's big wooden-framed windows—an official rite of spring, like Opening Day in baseball. Boxleiter was reclining in his chair, drinking in a breeze that was somehow still sweet after negotiating miles of city streets.

The editor was relaxing but not relaxed. He pushed the reason for his unease across the desktop to me, a clipping from page one of that morning's paper. I could tell the story was from page one because it was set next to the box containing the index and the morning chuckle and the prayer of the day.

The story's headline read "Was there postage due?" It had a subhead, too: "Elmwood mail arrives a little late." I'd read the story that morning. I reread it now to the accompaniment of paper on Boxleiter's desk rustling in the urban breeze.

The story began with a predictable joke lead about late mail: "Before launching your next tirade on the subject of slow mail service, stop and think of poor Elmwood." The meat of the story was contained in the next three paragraphs. In 1985, Virginia A. Chalmer, an Elmwood resident, sent a condolence card to Earl and Lily Tatum, also of Elmwood, whose son had passed away. Just last week—twelve years after the card was originally mailed—it was returned to Chalmer marked "addressee deceased, return to sender."

The next day, one of Chalmer's neighbors received a postcard that relatives vacationing in North Carolina had sent—in 1974.

Chalmer called the Tatum's surviving daughter, Mildred, to ask why the condolence card had been returned. Mildred denied ever seeing the card but added a third piece to the puzzle. That very day she had received a postcard with a 1965 postmark. It had been mailed from California by her brother Paul, the man whose death in 1985 had prompted Chalmer's letter of condolence.

The rest of the article consisted of denials and half-explanations from the Postal Service, some of them contradictory. The Elmwood postmaster kicked the matter upstairs, noting that mail for Elmwood is sorted in Muncie. The Muncie supervisor acknowledged that a piece of sorting equipment had been moved recently, but claimed that no letters had been found as a result. The director of communications for the Muncie district, who evidently hadn't compared stories with the supervisor, was quoted as saying that mail might have been found when the machine was moved, that the find might not have been reported if it was small, and that the eventual delivery of the mail was "an example of the dogged determination of the service."

The story had been submitted by a "special correspondent," which was byline code for a stringer, a local who didn't actually work for the *Star Republic* but occasionally submitted articles.

I read the piece through twice and then turned to the index box to read the prayer for the day: "Thank you Lord for this day and for reminding us that today is all we have." That didn't cheer me up, so I tried the morning chuckle: "If you think talk is cheap, you never called one of those telephone sex numbers."

By then Boxleiter had figured out that I was stalling. He repeated himself, something he liked to do: "What are the odds of that happening? That's the real story, and we didn't even mention it. We ran a Post-Office-screws-up-again piece. The real story's not even touched."

Boxleiter waited for me to name the hidden kernel of story, but I outlasted him. "How can it be a coincidence," he asked, "that these items of mail that happened to slip behind a sorting machine—one in 1965, one in 1974, and one in 1985—were all addressed to one little town?"

I was tempted to say that other little towns in the area might have received their own late deliveries, little towns that lacked a "special correspondent." But I knew that Boxleiter's question was just a trap, that he had yet to mention the really incalculable coincidence.

He mentioned it now. "What are the odds of two of the three pieces of mail—sent twenty years apart—would have a connection to one man, Paul Tatum?"

The breeze kicked up, sending the clipping across Boxleiter's desk. One end of it was snagged by a souvenir ashtray. The other end waved at us. Boxleiter settled deeper in his chair. "The redbud should be blooming around Elmwood," he said. "Let me know."

• • •

I drove out the next day, taking I-69 as far north as Pendleton and then switching to a state road with an unlucky designation: thirteen. The redbud trees were not blooming, but they were thinking about it. The daffodils were out in farmhouse yards, and the patches of woods between the fields were carpeted with tiny white wild flowers. The name of the flower was "Spring Beauty," but it could just as easily have been "Late Snow."

Elmwood was a crossroads town formed by the intersection of State Roads 13 and 28. There was a business district where the roads met, or what was left of a business district. The only really going concern was one of the antique malls that every small town in Indiana seemed to have acquired overnight.

The directions I'd obtained by phone that morning took me a mile or so down State Road 28 to a supermarket where the *Star Republic*'s special correspondent, R.T. Dunfee, worked as a bagger.

Dunfee was a teenager who planned to study journalism at Indiana University, starting in the fall. As he told me that, I wondered how much of his enthusiasm would survive until graduation. Enough, I decided, to carry him a few years into a career. His eyes glowed with the true fire, even shaded as they were by his ball cap's carefully creased brim. He wore a bow tie at the collar of his white short-sleeved shirt. The tie was part of his bagger's uniform, but it suited him. The tie and his reddish hair and his larger-than-life ears gave him a Jimmy Olsen quality that I liked.

"I got the tip for the story right here," he said, indicating the supermarket, a Shop-n-Bag. We were standing in the store's parking lot, which Dunfee jokingly called his office. "You get most of your big scoops in a town like this at the market."

You did until you were old enough to frequent bars, I thought.

"Mrs. Chalmer told me about it herself. She's the lady who sent the condolence letter in '85 that just came back. Mrs. Chalmer arranged for me to speak with her neighbor, who just got the postcard mailed in 1974. She tried to get me in to see Mildred Tatum, the lady who was supposed to get the postcard from her brother in 1965, only it just came. But Ms. Tatum wouldn't see me. I landed the interviews with the Post Office people myself."

I congratulated him on that initiative, while wondering if he'd worn the ball cap and tie to those interviews.

Dunfee was arranging sheets of paper on the hood of my car. There were three of them, photocopies of the delayed pieces of mail. I asked how he'd managed to get a complete set, since Mildred Tatum had refused to see him.

"Our postmaster, Hardy Smith, asked for copies after word of the late deliveries got around town. Ms. Tatum didn't turn down the Post Office.

"This one is hers, the postcard from 1965 from her brother Paul. The picture side was a photo of the ocean and some cliffs. You can see the postmark clearly. It was mailed from Monterey, California, on September 4." Not trusting my eyesight, Dunfee read the message to me. "'Loving it out here already. Feel like I'm home. Miss you. Love, Paul.'"

Dunfee had arranged his evidence chronologically. The 1974 postcard was next. It was addressed to a couple named

Seybert. The message was literally "Wish you were here." It was signed "Frank and Helen." The postmark was from Wilmington, North Carolina.

"That one had a picture of a battleship on the front," Dunfee said. "The USS *North Carolina.*"

The final photocopy was of a sheet of notepaper that had once been folded into thirds. It was the letter of condolence, dated June 20, 1985, written by Virginia Chalmer, and addressed to the Tatums. The note mentioned the recent death of their son Paul, but contained no particulars. Extending below the Xeroxed image was a tiny flap with a ragged edge. I asked Dunfee about it.

"That's the seal that held the note together." He dug in his pocket. "Mr. Smith copied the other side, too, so he could get the postmark. The note was written on special card stock that came with the folds already in it. You wrote the note, folded it up, sealed it with this little wafer thing, and put the address and stamp on the outside. See? I've never seen one like this before, but Mrs. Chalmer said she used to use them all the time.

"Do you think it could have gotten hung up in some sorting machine because the sides were open?"

Dunfee still had the big story in sight, the sins of the Post Office, but then, he hadn't been reassigned by Boxleiter. I asked if he minded my doing some digging, and he gave me directions to Virginia Chalmer's home and the copies of the three pieces of mail, assuring me that he had other copies tucked away in a safe place. I'd already guessed that.

Mrs. Chalmer lived in a limestone ranch two blocks from the Shop-n-Bag. Her door was answered by a visiting nurse whose visit was just ending. The nurse showed me into the living room, where Mrs. Chalmer sat in a Queen Anne chair, dressed as though she was expecting the chair's namesake to show up for tea. The nurse listened while I introduced myself and asked Mrs. Chalmer if she'd grant me an interview. When the old woman said yes, the nurse picked up her bag, placed a sweater around Mrs. Chalmer's shoulders, and showed herself out.

Mrs. Chalmer had been a teacher, as I might have guessed from her strong voice and careful diction. She told me about her teaching career, the length of time she'd lived in Elmwood—forty-four years—and what her late husband had died of—a stroke. All that before she returned to the subject of her wayward condolence card. She confirmed what Dunfee had written in his article, adding that she'd happened to hear of the Seyberts' much delayed postcard from North Carolina from the visiting nurse.

"I learned of the postcard from California that had never reached poor Mildred Tatum when I called to ask her about my note to her parents. You knew that from the newspaper article. Mildred stayed on in the family house after her parents passed on within a few months of each other last year. I called her to ask why she hadn't kept my card herself, why she hadn't even broken the seal. She said she'd never seen the card, never written 'addressee dead, return to sender' on it. How that happened is a mystery. I asked my mail person, Mr. Clark, about that. He said he hadn't written that on the card. He's Mildred Tatum's carrier, too. I should have mentioned that."

I asked Mrs. Chalmer how long Clark had been her letter carrier. "A little over a year, I think. So I couldn't expect him to know anything about the card. I've teased him about it, though. Everyone on his route has, poor boy. He said he couldn't even remember bringing it to me. He wouldn't, though, would he? Not with all the catalogs and junk mail."

I asked if I could see the original of the condolence card.

"Sorry. Mildred asked me for it, so I sent it on. She won't show it to you, I'm afraid. She won't even see you. She's cross with me about the newspaper article."

When I asked why, Mrs. Chalmer gave a little shrug that caused her sweater to slip off one shoulder. While she replaced it, she kept her eyes fixed on mine. I had the impression she was watching me for a particular response.

"It's funny," she said. "It's been twelve years since I wrote that note, but I still remember doing it. When I found it in my little mail box last week, I knew right away what it was. So sad to lose a child."

Mrs. Chalmer insisted on seeing me to the door. She used her walker to steady herself when she stood. Then she carried it as she walked, holding it out before her like the handlebars of an imaginary bicycle. She didn't set it down until we reached her front door.

There, I paused to ask how Paul Tatum had died.

Mrs. Chalmer leaned on the walker until its aluminum frame creaked. "AIDS, poor boy," she said.

I had no trouble finding the Tatum house; I had the address on the photocopied postcard from the dead Paul Tatum and I'd seen the street name, Shelby, on my drive from the Shop-n-Bag. Getting inside the house, a neat Arts and Crafts cottage, was another matter. I rang the bell and knocked and heard someone moving about in the front room, but the door never opened.

I went next to the local post office to interview the postmaster, Hardy Smith. He was a big man near retirement age who was more sedentary—from what I saw of him—than Mrs. Chalmer. He resembled the old woman in another way: He gave me the impression he was privately urging me to guess a secret. From the very start of the interview he leaned forward and watched me with the expectant attitude of a man who had a pea hidden under a walnut shell.

"Thought someone might be back about those letters," Smith said. "That Dunfee boy's a bright kid, comes from a real nice family, but he's easily distracted. I only had to mention the sorting center in Muncie, and he was off. It was just bad luck for Dunfee that they'd actually moved some equipment over there. That really derailed him. He never did see the most interesting thing about those three pieces of mail."

He paused to let me fill in the blank. Earlier in the day, I would have answered with the coincidence that fascinated Boxleiter: two of the three pieces of mail had a connection to Paul Tatum. But I'd now seen reproductions of the mail, and I'd recognized something that all three pieces had in common. They all could be read by anyone who handled them, the postcards because they were postcards and the condolence card because it had open ends. A nosy person could press the card's top and bottom together, bowing the sides outward and winning a glimpse of at least part of the message.

I shared this observation with Smith, and he rewarded me with a smile. But that was all. He didn't volunteer anything else, not even another hint. To fill the silence, I repeated what Mrs. Chalmer had said about having a new letter carrier.

Smith leaned forward a little more as he answered. "Time must pass quickly for her. Clark's had the route for almost two years now."

I asked who had had the route before Clark, Smith almost nodding his encouragement as I worded the question.

"A fellow named Wilbur Dirr," Smith said. "His father, Waylon Dirr, had been a mailman, too. Not a letter carrier, sir, a mailman. Waylon was a legend in this office. Never missed a day, never used a jeep or a truck. Wilbur was almost as steady, which is saying something in this day and age."

I asked when Wilbur had started at the Postal Service.

"Nineteen sixty-five. Right out of high school. Never wanted to be anything but a mailman. I remember it was '65 because we made a big to-do over his thirtieth anniversary when it came around in '95. I don't know that Wilbur liked that very much. Wasn't a big one for fussing. But he didn't have much family, just his widowed mother who kept house for him, or many friends, so we decided to do the right thing by him. We were glad we did, too, sir, because just a few months later he was dead and buried."

I asked how Dirr had died. Smith pretended not to understand the question.

"Died while he was doing his route, just the way you'd expect Waylon Dirr's son to go. In harness. Or did you mean what did he die of? Heart attack, which is just what you would have expected Wilbur to have, if you'd known him. He was a man who saved his emotions the way a squirrel saves nuts. Wilbur kept every feeling he ever had. Buried them, buried them inside. Every secret he ever had, too."

I asked Smith if he had anything official to say about the likelihood that Wilbur Dirr had withheld the three pieces of mail. While I was at it, I asked the postmaster if he had an opinion on how those three cards had gotten themselves delivered almost two years after Dirr's death.

Smith didn't laugh at me for asking. He didn't answer me, either. Instead, he grew philosophical.

"You'll hear people say that small towns are intolerant. I don't believe that's true of Elmwood. In fact, sir, I sometimes think just the opposite, that Elmwood can be too tolerant, by which I mean that we can use tolerance as an excuse for plain laziness and indifference, for letting a person struggle on alone, for not getting involved. A family can be that way, too. And after all, sir, what is a small town but an extended family?"

I stood up, wondering how I might still tie the undelivered mail to Wilbur Dirr. It came to me that the key was the piece that didn't fit the pattern, the piece that didn't refer to Paul Tatum. As the still expectant Smith watched me, I tried to visualize the postcard sent to Mrs. Chalmer's neighbors, the Seyberts, in 1974, the postcard with the innocuous message and the picture of the ship on the front, the USS *North Carolina.*

I asked Smith if Waylon Dirr, Wilbur's father, had ever been in the service.

"Seems to me he was," Smith said. "Now that you mention it. The navy, I believe."

I had no trouble finding the former home of Wilbur Dirr. His widowed mother still lived there, as Smith had mentioned conversationally as we'd said our good-byes. He'd also let slip Mrs. Dirr's address, but I had the feeling that I could have found her bungalow without Smith's help, that each of the contracting circles I'd traveled had had the little house as its center.

Mrs. Dirr must have watched me climb the walk to her door; she opened it that quickly. She was short and heavy, the latter quality accentuated by her velour sweat suit. She might have been the same age as Mrs. Chalmer; it was difficult to tell. There were still traces of black in her gray hair. On the tip of her sharp chin, a single black hair had grown long enough to curl. "Yes?" she said.

I showed Mrs. Dirr my press card. While she was studying it, I produced the photocopies Dunfee had given me. Mrs. Dirr wasn't surprised to see them.

"I was afraid you might be from the Postal Service," she said with genuine relief. "Come in if you want to."

She showed me into a living room whose furniture all wore crocheted covers.

"I saw that article in your paper," she said. "I was sorry that you blamed it on the Postal Service. I never meant for that to happen. You should write that down. I have a world of respect for the United States Postal Service. My husband taught me that. He took his job very seriously. So did my son," she added a touch hastily. "You can write that down, too."

I hadn't written anything down so far. I hadn't even taken out my notebook. I asked her when she had found the undelivered mail.

"Just last week," she answered indignantly. "Just before I

delivered it. I would never have held on to it. I was going through some of my son's things. I didn't do much of that when he passed on. Respected his privacy even then. But now I'm giving up the house, so I had to. Too much work, this house.

"I found the mail in Wilbur's desk. I don't know why he kept it. It must have been a mistake."

I asked her if her son had known Paul Tatum.

"Of course he did. Weren't they in the same grade all through school? Weren't they best friends? Leastways Wilbur thought they were. He hated it when Paul moved out West. Wilbur looked for mail from him, but there never was any. I told him that any friend who could forget him that fast wasn't worth mooning over. Wilbur's life was here, and it was a good life."

Though a little short, I thought. I asked Mrs. Dirr if her husband had served on the *North Carolina*.

"Yes. That must have been why Wilbur kept that postcard," she added, forgetting her earlier claim that it had all been a mistake. "He and his father never shared much—except the Postal Service. Wilbur kept those other things because of Paul Tatum, I expect. Because they'd been friends. Good friends."

I decided that she was telling me exactly what she believed to be true, and that brought to mind something Postmaster Smith had said about families and how little help they sometimes were. Though Mrs. Dirr remembered her son being anxious for some word of Tatum in 1965, she evidently had no idea why Dirr had considered himself the proper recipient of a condolence card when Tatum died twenty years later. I decided I'd been wrong when I'd classified Dirr's life as short. That can't have been the way it had seemed to him.

My extended silence had an unintended effect on Mrs. Dirr, making her talkative. "I sealed back up that card from Mrs. Chalmer. Wilbur—or someone, I mean—had peeled off the wafer that held it together. I glued it back. I marked it 'addressee deceased,' because I knew the Tatums had passed on, too. I put the card in Mrs. Chalmer's mailbox one day just after the carrier had been there. I delivered the two postcards the same way, but on different days because I had to wait and watch for the letter carrier at each house."

I stood up to take my leave. Mrs. Dirr seemed disappointed with me, perhaps because I hadn't written down a word of her confession. To make it up to her, I asked her a final question: Why hadn't she simply destroyed the three pieces of mail?

"You can't hold on to things," she said. "It's wrong to do that. It hurts everyone, keeping things from being delivered. I know that now."

I didn't apologize to Mrs. Dirr for underestimating her, but I should have. I thanked her instead for her time and headed south for Indy.

THE VIGIL

That my editor's parents loved Christmas was reflected in the name they gave their only child: Emanuel Noel. Their son's feelings for the holiday might be deduced from his having used only his first two initials and his last name all his adult life: E.N. Boxleiter.

Those of us who worked for him at an Indianapolis daily called the *Star Republic* didn't have to guess about Boxleiter's opinion of Christmas. We were used to his temper growing shorter as December's days did, used to him delegating anything to do with the holiday, used to his annual attempts to tone down and dry out the office Christmas parties, attempts that were frustrated by the family that owned the paper.

So I was a little surprised when Boxleiter called me into his office early one Christmas Eve and told me he had a special Christmas assignment for me.

"It's that little girl who's praying for the miracle roof. You know the one."

I did. The little girl's name was Tina Vasquez. She was a third grader at St. Mary's Catholic School, which belonged to an old parish of the same name located on the east side of downtown Indianapolis. Tina was the darling of the media for the second year in a row. Video of her kneeling before a statue of the Blessed Virgin in old St. Mary's was running on local television stations almost every night. Sometimes she was alone, sometimes she was flanked by classmates, the girls dressed as they had for their First Communion ceremony, in white dresses and white veils.

They were praying for a Christmas present and a large one: a new roof for the old church. A miracle roof, as Boxleiter had called it. It would have been an impossible long shot, except that, exactly one Christmas earlier, Tina had prayed up an entire automobile single-handed.

Or maybe not single-handed, since the *Star Republic* had played a small part. The pastor of St. Mary's had called in the story. The priest had explained that Tina was the only child of a single mother and that the two of them were just getting by on welfare. The mother had a chance for a good job, but she needed a car. So Tina had begun a marathon prayer session before a statue of Mary, praying for a Christmas miracle.

And she'd gotten one. We'd run Tina's picture and story two days before Christmas. On Christmas morning, the

Vasquez family had awakened to find a late model Saturn parked outside their double, its title and keys in their mailbox. The local television stations had made it one of the most videotaped cars in Indiana. The *Star Republic*, the paper that had launched the story, hadn't published so much as a black-and-white photo.

"I was afraid last year that we'd created a monster," Boxleiter now said. "That's why I killed the follow-up story, not that it did any good. Here the kid is, back again, praying away. St. Mary's has already received thousands of dollars in contributions. At the rate the money's coming in, they'll be able to shingle that roof in five dollar bills."

I asked what was wrong with that.

"Nothing, if it's all legitimate. If it's a scam, it's our fault for getting it started. I want you to check it out."

There didn't seem to me to be much to check out. The money was going directly to the parish, so the Vasquez family couldn't be profiting.

When I pointed that out to Boxleiter, he snapped, "Even if this year's money is going to a church, next year's money might not. Some soppy idiot gives a car away, and who knows where it will lead?"

To get an additional rise out of him and to pay him back a little for sending me out into the cold on the day of the office Christmas parties, I asked if he was sure the Saturn hadn't come from the Blessed Virgin.

He waved me out of his office. "Prove it did," he said, "and you can have my Christmas bonus."

The drive to St. Mary's was so short my car heater never awoke from its nap. The church was one of downtown Indy's most beautiful, a happy marriage of French Gothic architecture and Indiana limestone. As I parked in its shadow, I was struck for the hundredth time by the irony that the poorest parishes always had the oldest churches, the ones with the highest maintenance tabs. Luckily for St. Mary's, it also had Tina Vasquez.

She was hard at it, a little girl in a white dress, her long brown hair partially hidden by a gauzy white veil. She was flanked by a girl and a boy, the boy in a white shirt and dark blue dress pants, surely the school uniform. Several other children sat in nearby pews with their parents, awaiting their shifts.

Tina knelt with a perfectly straight back, her tiny hands together but not interlocked. The day was overcast, and the church under lit. As a result, most of the light on Tina's face came from banks of flickering candles before the statue of the Virgin. The candlelight emphasized the girl's dominant feature, her very large, very dark eyes. Those eyes were fixed on the statue before her, which had Mary, in her traditional blue and white, standing on a blue globe that was covered in golden stars.

I'd walked all the way up the center aisle of the church, almost to the altar, so I could view the little girl's face as unobtrusively as possible. That wasn't unobtrusive enough for the priest who intercepted me and asked me my business. When I showed him my press card, he ushered in into the sacristy, a little room off the altar, apologizing as we went.

"I'm sorry if I was rude, but we've been getting a lot of gawkers, thanks to the television coverage. This morning, a woman actually tried to get Tina's autograph."

I thought of pointing out that the parish was also getting a new roof thanks to the television coverage. Instead I asked how close they were to their goal.

"We're almost there," the priest, whose name was Marcelli, said. He was a young man with large, out-of-focus eyes and a tendency to draw certain words out as though he were chanting them. "It's quite remarkable. We're expecting an extra large crowd for tonight's midnight mass, because Tina will be ending her vigil then. The collection should put us over the top."

I asked him how long he had known the Vasquez family.

"I baptized Tina. It was just after I was assigned here to St. Mary's. Tina's mother, Marguerite, is a sweet woman, but she's had more than her share of problems. It's the old story, I'm afraid. She fell in love with a guy who promised her the world and only came through with a baby. After he'd gotten her pregnant, the guy, Tony Donica, hung around for a while. He and Marguerite lived together and there was talk of them getting married. Then Donica found another young woman who believed his line. They ran off together to Las Vegas. Something happened out there, an accident or something; I'm not sure of the details. And I know you didn't come here to listen to old gossip."

His unfocused eyes grew slightly sharper. "Exactly why have you come? I have to say that I've been a little disappointed with the *Star Republic*. I was the one who called the story in to you last year. You ran a nice little article about Tina before Christmas, but nothing after the car arrived. And nothing so far this year. I was sure you'd forsaken us."

I paraphrased Boxleiter's concerns about the potential for abuse in the phenomenon the *Star Republic* had gotten started.

"You needn't be worried," the priest assured me. "This is the last year for the vigil. Tina and her mother both told me that. Tina only did it this year as a thank you for the car. The Blessed Virgin came through for Tina last year, so Tina wanted to do something in return. A new roof for Our Lady's church is a pretty big something, but that's the kind of special kid she is."

I asked Marcelli if he really believed the car had come from the Virgin.

He laughed. "Not directly. I know it was some kind soul who read your paper's article and felt a welling up of Christmas spirit. But who's to say what caused that spirit to well up? Tina believes it was the intercession of Mary, and so do I."

He suddenly took me by the arm. "Listen. The thing for

you to do is to meet Marguerite. That will put your mind at rest. She's just down the hall in the room the Altar Rosary Society uses. Her mother-in-law, Tina's grandmother, is there, too. I know there was no marriage so there can't be a mother-in-law, but Marguerite calls Mrs. Donica that, so I do, too."

He led me down a hallway whose wooden floor not only creaked but also cracked and popped. The women in the Altar Rosary room couldn't help but be aware of our approach. There were two of them, seated at a card table that held coffee cups and a plate of Christmas cookies. The younger one, Marguerite, was a future portrait of Tina. She had the girl's dark eyes and slightly upturned nose, though the effect of the eyes was diminished by a much fuller face. The older woman's face was very spare, and her eyes were narrowed by a skeptical, put-upon expression. I hated to think of Tina ever looking at the world in that sharp, cynical way.

After he'd introduced us, Father Marcelli excused himself and left. The awkwardness that followed wasn't lifted by the grandmother's opening remark.

"So, your newspaper is finally interested in Tina again now that it's sure she'll make it. You didn't have the faith to come a week ago even."

I pointed out that we'd had faith enough to run the original story about Tina, and that led us into a discussion of the prior Christmas's miracle, the car. Marguerite gave me the whole story again, speaking without a trace of the older woman's accent. Her voice did get husky, though, when she mentioned Tina's father. Oddly, Donica's own mother was much less sentimental.

"That one," she all but sneered. "He'd be alive today if he'd married you like he should have and stayed with you like he should have. He had a good job at the Methodist Hospital. He could have supported you and Tina. But no. He runs away to Las Vegas with some fat blonde, drives drunk, and gets them both killed."

Mrs. Donica made the sign of the cross when she mentioned her son's fatal accident. She'd performed the same ritual earlier in her tirade, when she'd used the words "he'd be alive today."

Marguerite calmly ignored the older woman. "The car turned everything around for us. You should have seen it shining in the sun on Christmas morning. So pretty. When I found the title and the keys in my mailbox, I couldn't believe it. I cried and cried. Thanks to my little Saturn, I have a good job. Tina and I have our own place and our own life."

She went on to describe the color of the car—red—and its reliability and mileage—both miraculous. I was happy to dwell on the subject of the Saturn. As Father Marcelli had predicted, meeting Marguerite Vasquez had settled any doubts I'd inherited from my editor regarding the propriety of little Tina's fundraising. But there remained the challenge

Boxleiter had tossed me as I'd left his office: proving the car had come from the Blessed Mother.

I asked Marguerite if she remembered the name of the previous owner of the Saturn, which would have appeared above hers on the title document she'd found in her mailbox.

Mrs. Donica thrust herself across the table, her arm extended, her palm flat. "Don't tell him," she said. "Don't say another word. He wants to tell people it wasn't a miracle, that it wasn't the Virgin Mary."

I told Marguerite what the priest had told me, that identifying the human donor wouldn't prove that Mary wasn't behind the miracle. The donor might even confirm that she was. But it was a waste of my time. Her mother-in-law's outstretched arm and upturned palm had sealed her lips. I would never hear another word from Marguerite Vasquez.

I thanked them for the interview and started to leave. Then I decided to test a little theory I'd come up with. I turned and said that it was a shame Tony Donica hadn't lived to see the good his daughter was doing.

Marguerite only nodded sadly, but Mrs. Donica made the sign of the cross for the third time.

Once outside in the cold, I started my Chevy and we sat there shaking together. While the engine warmed, I placed a call to the *Star Republic*, to the cubicle of Eric Neuman, once an unpromising copyboy and now the paper's specialist in computer research, legitimate and not so.

"Where are you?" he asked before I could say more than my name. "The Christmas parties are starting up. The one in Home Delivery is going full bore. They'll be dancing on their desktops by two."

I told him I was on a special assignment for Boxleiter and that I needed to find a man named Tony Donica. The theory I'd carried away from the Altar Rosary room was that Donica was still alive. That was my interpretation of Mrs. Donica's habit of blessing herself every time someone mentioned her son's death. She didn't seem the type to be praying for the repose of that black sheep's soul. So I'd started to wonder if her signs of the cross might be little acts of contrition for an ongoing lie.

"Have you got anything besides a name?" Neuman asked. "It's a big country, and somebody spiked my eggnog."

I related the little I knew of Donica: He'd supposedly been in an automobile accident in Las Vegas and he'd once worked at Methodist Hospital.

"Bingo," Neuman said. "I've got a buddy over at Methodist. He can get me Donica's Social Security Number. With that, it'll be easy. Give me twenty minutes."

I bought lunch at a drive-through White Castle on South Street, thinking as I paid of all the free food I was missing at the office pitch-ins. Before I'd finished my last burger, my mobile rang.

"Got him," Neuman said. "He's receiving disability

payments from Social Security. But I hope he's not trying to live on what they're sending him."

I asked where in Nevada the checks were being delivered, though I was secretly hoping that his address was nearer to home.

"He's back in Indiana. In Greenfield, of all places. Maybe he's a James Whitcomb Riley fan."

That Hoosier poet's hometown was a thirty minute drive east of Indianapolis. A short drive, in other words, but long enough for me to sketch out the rest of my Christmas story. I was seeing Donica as the mystery donor of the Saturn. How he'd managed it on his disability checks, I had no idea. Maybe he'd had some money left from an insurance settlement. I also didn't know why he was pretending to be dead. The reasons I considered included Donica's ongoing remorse over having deserted his wife and child and the possibility that he had been horribly disfigured in the accident. I was pulling for the remorse angle because the fairy-tale ending I saw for the story was a holiday reconciliation of Tony and Marguerite, brought about by the divine intercession of the *Star Republic*.

The address Neuman had given me belonged to an old building not far from Greenfield's courthouse square. The structure resembled a two-story army barracks, though it had been covered in some kind of composite material intended by its manufacturer to look like shake shingles. Extremely large and extremely flat shake shingles. The building had a fire escape on each end and other indications that it was an apartment building, but no sign giving its name. The names of the tenants appeared on a row of rural mailboxes wired to a wooden fence. Tony Donica occupied apartment 1B.

Donica was in, but not receiving visitors. When I knocked on his door, it opened only as wide as its security chain would permit, which, luckily for me, wasn't as wide as the muzzle of the rottweiler that tried to bull its way out. Behind the door, in the shadows, I could just see Donica, his face a little lower than my chest, the height of a man in a wheelchair.

"What the hell do you want?" he demanded, the words so slurred I knew he was as drunk as the revelers back at the *Star Republic*.

I identified myself and told him I wanted to talk about his daughter. He then offered to sell me an interview. Twenty dollars for five minutes. I passed the money in.

We talked in Donica's combination living room, dining room, and bedroom, a dank, dirty place that made me glad I hadn't sprung for the ten-minute interview. Donica had lost both legs above the knee, and the only clear spaces in the apartment were the pathways he used to wheel his chair from his unmade bed to his cluttered table or out to his bathroom or kitchenette.

"What about Tina?" he asked to get the clock running. "Something happen to her?"

I could see a trace of the good looks that had won the hearts of Marguerite and the ill-fated, unnamed blonde, though his chin was unshaved and his hair both unwashed and uncombed.

I told him I'd come about the car Tina had prayed for and gotten for Christmas. Donica's expression conveyed as much comprehension as that of the dog seated beside him.

"Why would a little brat need a car?"

I told him it had been a present for her mother.

"That bitch," Donica said. "What kind of car?" And, when I'd told him, "A piece of crap. I had a Trans Am."

He pointed to a framed photo of a gleaming black car. I looked around for a picture of Tina, but didn't spot one.

I started to tell him about the roof Tina was praying for.

Donica cut in with, "What do you care about some church in Milwaukee?"

It was my turn to look blank.

"Milwaukee," Donica repeated, sounding out the word as though for a child. "Where that fireman Tina married took her and the brat. My mother told me all about it, so don't think I don't know."

By then, I was starting to realize the extent of what Donica didn't know. He didn't know that Tina and Marguerite were still in Indianapolis. He didn't know about last year's Christmas miracle or this year's. That didn't seem possible after all the airtime the Indianapolis television stations had devoted to the story. Their signals carried to Greenfield easily. I gave the apartment a closer examination. There was no television in sight.

When I asked Donica about that, he said, "I hate television. People on television have legs." He added, a little defensively, "I've got a great stereo. With satellite radio. No commercials."

No local news, either. That left the original newspaper story about Tina, the one that had produced the car. The *Star Republic* sold a suburban edition in Greenfield. I asked Donica if he ever saw the paper.

"Waste of good beer money," he said.

When I'd first heard that Donica had chosen to settle in little Greenfield, I'd thought it was part of his plan to pass himself off as dead. Now it seemed that the remote location had to be part of someone else's plan. Donica confirmed that when I asked him about his apartment.

"My mom got me this place cheap. One of her old hen friends owns the building. If I had the money, I'd have a place in Indy. On South Meridian, where all the bars are. There isn't a bar in this town worth wheeling myself to."

So the same woman who had lied to her son about Marguerite marrying and moving north had tucked Donica away at a safe distance. That was to protect the lie she'd told him and the one she'd told Marguerite, namely that her son had died in Las Vegas. Without a television or a newspaper or a neighborhood bar, he was as isolated as he would have been on the moon. His mother could let her granddaughter have a week of celebrity without worrying too much about Donica finding out.

I was wondering how to break the truth to him when he said, "You never answered me. Why does your paper care about some church in Milwaukee? You said the brat's praying for a roof. The little bitch. She's a chip off the old bitch block I bet. If she'd got an in with God, she should be praying for new legs for her old man. I'd shake them out of her if I could get my hands on her.

"You said you came here because of the car she prayed for. Why? You expect me to cry for you because I didn't get one?"

My theory seemed ridiculous now, but I'd spent twenty bucks to confirm it, so I ran it by him.

Donica laughed himself into a hacking fit. "You think I bought that car for Marguerite? You think if I had the money for a car I'd waste it on that bitch? Is she here taking care of me like a woman's supposed to? Hell no. She's in Milwaukee, screwing some goddamn fireman. If only I'd married her like she begged me to. Me and Zeus would have that bitch walking around here on her knees." He rubbed the dog's head vigorously. "Wouldn't we, boy?"

So much for my bright idea about the Saturn. That left the Christmas miracle I'd been contemplating, the reuniting of Tina and her mother with Donica. The thought that I'd almost done that, had almost blurted out to Donica that Marguerite believed him dead, literally made me dizzy. I felt as though I were standing on the edge of a cliff with one foot in the air.

Donica snapped me out of it by saying, "Your time's up. Get out of here or I'll have Zeus chase you out."

I drove back downtown, intending to join the *Star Republic*'s Christmas parties, now well underway. But when I got off the interstate, I drove to St. Mary's. I still wanted to find the person who had donated the car. More than that, I wanted to hear the person say that a vision of the Virgin or a surplus of Dickensian Christmas spirit had motivated the gift. I no longer cared what the motive was, as long as it was positive. I needed something to counteract the darkness I'd found in Greenfield. But to locate the mystery donor, I had to do something dark myself.

On my earlier visit, I'd left St. Mary's by a back door very near the rectory. I tried that door now and found it unlocked. On my way to the Altar Rosary room I worked out strategies for separating Marguerite and Mrs. Donica, but I didn't need one. The "mother-in-law" was seated alone in the little room, knitting.

It was a picture worthy of the front of a greeting card, but when the woman looked up and saw me, her expression instantly soured and the needles she held suddenly looked as dangerous as her son's dog.

"What are you doing back here?" she demanded.

I told her I'd just been to Greenfield, and that was enough. She was out of her seat so fast she might have stabbed me before I'd raised a hand, if she'd headed for me and not the door.

"You can't tell Marguerite," she said when she had it safely closed. "You can't. She'd run to him, and that would be the end of her and her better life. I know. I lived with Tony's father for twenty years. And Tony's worse." She blessed herself again. "It isn't just his legs. It's him. I won't let Marguerite sacrifice herself. I won't let little Tina live like that, maybe grow up like that herself."

I told Mrs. Donica that it might not be necessary for me to speak to Marguerite. I only wanted the name of the previous owner of the Saturn. Mrs. Donica could tell me that herself.

She understood the bargain at once: Give me the donor's name and let the *Star Republic* take some of the glitter away from the original miracle, or I would tell Marguerite everything. It was a bluff, but she didn't call it.

"It wasn't a person," she said, her voice flat and tired. "It was a company. Friendly Motors. In Terre Haute."

Halfway to the door, I turned and asked her why she'd let Tina risk a second vigil. There was always the chance some friend of Donica's might pass him the word.

"I didn't want it to happen again," she said. "But I could never say no to her."

I thought she meant Tina. Then she glanced toward an old painting of a smiling woman in blue, and I was no longer sure.

Terre Haute was farther west of Indianapolis than

Greenfield was east. I tried phoning Friendly Motors from my car, got a busy signal, and decided to make the drive. If my call had gone through, I never would have learned the truth, because the man who knew the answer, Marshall Henson, owner and manager of Friendly Motors, intended to take the secret to his grave.

Henson made that clear to me before he'd finished shaking my hand. "Swore I'd never tell a soul and I never will," he said as he ushered me into his tiny office. He was an older gentleman whose white hair and dentures shared an identical yellow tinge.

"That's the only Christmas miracle I've been involved with since I helped General Patton lift the siege of Bastogne in '44, and I'd hate to do anything to foul it up. Not that I don't tell the story of that Saturn to folks," he added, gesturing toward the wall to my right. "But I never tell the name of the man who bought the car."

The wall Henson had indicated was so cluttered with sales awards and group photos of dealership-sponsored softball teams that it took me a moment to spot something connected to Tina Vasquez. That something was a framed newspaper article describing how Tina and her mother had found the Saturn. The story was dated December 26 and carried the *Star Republic*'s name at the top. It was the work of a reporter I knew very well, a frustrated novelist named Joan Johnson.

"I insisted that the buyer send me a copy of whatever the

Indy paper ran about the car so I'd have a memento," Henson said. "Tell you the truth, I asked for the clipping so I'd be sure the guy hadn't been pulling my leg. I gave him a great deal on that car because of the story about the little girl—five thousand even for a really nice car—and I wanted to be sure he wasn't ripping me off.

"Anyway, he kept his side of the bargain, so I have to keep mine. Sorry you drove all the way over here for nothing."

I accepted his apology, even though my drive hadn't been for nothing. I'd seen a very rare thing, a Xerox copy of a newspaper article that had never run. Boxleiter himself had told me earlier that day that he'd personally killed the Vasquez follow-up story.

I drove back a little faster than I'd driven out. On the way, I placed a call to Joan Johnson. It took a while for the person who answered her phone to locate Joan. While I waited out the search, I listened to loud voices and laughter and even singing. I decided the office parties had reached their zenith, which Joan confirmed when she finally came on the line.

"Where are you? You're missing all the fun. In fact, you've missed most of it already."

I told her I was on my way in and asked if she remembered writing the second Tina Vasquez story.

"One of my better efforts," Joan said, "so of course it ended up in the trash. Boxleiter gave me the assignment himself, asked me to run him off a page proof. Then he told me he'd decided not to use it."

I asked her if she'd ever gotten her proof back.

"Why would I have wanted that? Anytime I need scrap paper, I just tear off a page of my novel. Hurry up back here. People are starting to sneak out."

I did hurry, but Joan had been right. By the time I reached the paper's employee parking lot, half the spaces were empty.

I nearly ran on my way inside. Then I did run up the stairs to the third floor, where the offices of the credit union were located. The lights were still on and two of the clerks, Dee and Lois, were still on duty, though both looked like they'd been at the Christmas cheer.

I walked in as casually as my shortness of breath would allow, wished them a happy holiday, and mentioned that someone in accounting had brought in a male stripper. They asked me to watch the phones and left abruptly.

So abruptly that Dee forgot to sign off her computer terminal, a serious breach of security. I sat down at it, located the records of Emanuel Noel Boxleiter, and learned that he'd made a sizable withdrawal exactly one year before. A five-thousand-dollar withdrawal.

Boxleiter was still in his darkened office, looking out at the lights of the park beneath his windows.

When he noticed me standing there, he asked, "So?"

I knew the question referred to his real concern, his reason for risking his secret by sending me out on the story. He was afraid, as the Friendly Motors man had been, that his leg had been pulled.

I told him the Vasquez family was as honest and deserving as they came. And that this was their last year in the miracle business.

He swung his chair around to face me. "What about the car? Did it come from the Virgin Mary after all?"

I shook my head. I told him it had come from St. Joseph, the guy who stood in the background and never got much credit.

Boxleiter grunted and said, "Maybe he never wanted any credit. Maybe just being a small part of some special kid's life was enough. Punch out and have a drink."

PASSAGE TO TAHITI

———

"Do you know how far it is from Indianapolis to Tahiti?"

I was used to E.N. Boxleiter, my editor at the *Star Republic*, a newspaper at the Indianapolis end of that hypothetical journey, beginning a conversation with a rhetorical question. So I waited him out. It wasn't a long wait.

"It's five thousand seven hundred and eighty miles by air. I looked it up." He pushed a section of that morning's paper across his scarred desktop. "Here's a guy who found a shortcut. Or something else. I'd like to know what exactly."

He'd passed me the Metro Region section, formerly called by the less snappy but more descriptive title City and State. A small article on its second page was circled in Boxleiter's trademark red ink. I was to do a follow-up, if I was reading the great man's mind correctly. Before I could ask for a verbal confirmation, a delegation of high school journalists was shown into Boxleiter's office. I slipped out, afraid he would use my example to scare them into careers in tax preparation.

Once I was safely back at my own desk, I read the red-ringed article. I should say I reread it. Its headline, "Remains may be those of man missing eighteen months," had caught my eye earlier that day. I didn't remember any mention of Tahiti in the accompanying story, though, and I didn't find one now, apart from a vague reference to "South Seas islands."

The focus of the article was one Douglas Dineen, sixty-two, a worker at a large home center, the Home Station, on Indy's south side. Dineen had gone missing eighteen months earlier, shortly after his doctor had found a spot on his left lung but before a diagnosis of cancer could be confirmed. He'd worked a full day following his doctor visit, but when his wife had come by the store to pick him up that evening, he could not be found.

The search for him had ranged as far west as Santa Fe, New Mexico, and as far north as the Canadian border. The scope was due to what seemed to be Dineen's defining characteristic: a wanderlust that everyone who knew him had mentioned. Dineen's wife, for example, had suggested that he might have gone to the American Southwest, a region that held a special fascination for him. A daughter had suggested the Boundary Waters area along the Canadian line. A coworker at the Home Station had spoken of faraway islands, unwittingly inspiring Boxleiter's research on Tahiti.

That same coworker, Joseph Albini, had later given the police the vital clue when they'd renewed their investigation at the eighteen-month anniversary of Dineen's disappearance. Albini had mentioned that Dineen would often spend his breaks staring out at a small field behind the store. The police had used a K9 unit to search the field and had found human bones, their condition consistent with exposure to the elements for a year and a half. Almost certainly, the bones were those of Douglas Dineen. The man who'd wanted to wander the globe hadn't made it a full quarter mile from the time clock he'd punched for years.

I spoke first by telephone with a policeman named Reiburg, whose chief concern seemed to be not appearing foolish in the pages of the *Star Republic*.

"Everybody we talked to told us that the guy was off somewhere hundreds of miles away, that he'd waited his whole life to travel. It made sense, too. He finds out he has a disease and—bam!—he takes off. The wife even passed on a claim by some family friends that they'd seen him in Santa Fe. We wasted time trying to confirm that and never could.

"All the staff at the Home Station gave us the same basic story, including Joseph Albini. He never said a word about Dineen staring out at that field until we came back eighteen months later and questioned him again. I'll tell you, if we'd found a bullet hole in that skull, I'd be talking to Mr. Albini pretty seriously right this minute. But there were no signs of foul play."

I asked about the cause of death, and Reiburg snorted into his end of the line.

"The forensics crew have what's left of the body. I don't know what they'll be able to figure out after all this time. Dineen probably died of exposure or thirst. Thirst, a hundred yards from the water cooler where he talked about all the great trips he was going to take. Figure that one out."

I next called the Home Station, learned that Joseph Albini was on duty that day, and set out. The store was a short drive from downtown on I-65. When I exited at Southport Road, the Home Station was already in sight, but getting to it proved a challenge. The strip mall containing the home store had been shoehorned into a triangle of land formed by the interstate, Southport Road, and Emerson Avenue. From what I could see of the result, squeezing the stores in had been easier than accommodating the extra traffic they brought. I had to wait through several lights on busy Southport and then make a left onto Emerson against stiff opposition.

At the Home Station's information desk, I was collected by a man whose name tag read "Grady." He was short and heavyset, a combination that gave him a slow, rolling gait. That in turn gave him plenty of time to bend my ear during our slow march to the back of the store.

"We can't stop talking around here about Doug passing

that way, me especially. I keep thinking of how Trigger, my old German shepherd, died a few years back. Trigger was the best dog I ever had, never a day of trouble until that last day. That was the day he disappeared. Happened to be a Sunday, and the whole family was over, which made it all the more odd, because Trigger was a real family dog. Anyway, we all spread out and combed the neighborhood, yelling his name and generally disturbing the Sabbath.

"And we couldn't find him. Well, it happened that my place was right next to a little field, an old soybean field they hadn't planted that year. Was going to be a new housing development, but they hadn't started yet. Some weeds had grown up, but they weren't too tall. You could stand in my yard and scan the whole field and see there was nothing in it, certainly not a dog that would come to you if you called to it. But one of my little nieces went out there anyway, and she found Trigger. He was just laying there in the weeds, sick. We took him right to our vet, who found a tumor. So I had him put down. When I heard about old Doug's body being out back, I naturally thought of Trigger."

It might have been a natural thought, but something about Grady's reminiscence bothered me. Maybe it was his smiling delivery or my impression that he was more moved by what had happened to his dog than by the death of his coworker.

So it was a relief to trade Grady's company for that of Joseph Albini. He was a young man with dark hair and eyes and olive skin and he couldn't think of Dineen, it seemed, without shaking his head.

"I wish I'd remembered about that field when the police first came around here," he said. "I can't believe I didn't."

I decided not to tell Albini that the police felt the same way about it. We were looking at the field as we spoke, standing in the very doorway where Douglas Dineen had often stood, according to Albini. It wasn't much of a view. The field was the undeveloped remnant of the land on which the mall had been built, and like the larger property, it was three-sided, those sides being I-65, the service road that ran behind the stores, and the right-of-way for some high-tension power lines. These lines cut across the landscape in seven-league strides, and the ground beneath them was mowed like a ball diamond. In contrast, the little plot that had fascinated Dineen was overgrown with weeds and, in its farthest corner, saplings.

Near that baby forest, an improvised barrier of crime-scene tape on sticks showed where the body had been found. It was no more than fifty yards from where we stood and perhaps twice that far from the chain-link fence that bordered the highway. No motorists had called to report a corpse, but that was understandable, as the roadbed was well below the level of the field. The difference in heights and the fringe of saplings had been all the screen Dineen had needed.

"This is right where he used to stand," Albini said,

shaking his head again. "He would smoke his cigarettes and talk about all the places he was going to go someday. Only he would talk about it backwards. I mean, not in the way you'd expect him to. He knew so much, it was like he was telling you about someplace he'd already been. He liked to look things up in books and he watched a lot of travel shows on television. If he'd ever made it to someplace like Bora Bora, he could have told the natives things. He could have been a tour guide."

I asked Albini if Dineen had seemed unhappy.

"Not when he was talking about being somewhere else."

As he said it, he looked around the stockroom behind us, inviting me to do the same. It was cavernous and dimly lit and smelled of forklift exhaust and sawdust. I thanked him for his time and exited though the back door. I crossed the service road and walked into Dineen's field, looking for the source of its strange attraction. All I got for my trouble were burrs on my socks.

My next stop was the Dineen family home in a nearby subdivision, Holiday Hills. I would have stopped there first, except that Dineen's widow, whom I'd reached by phone, had asked me to delay my visit until she could assemble her family. The gathering turned out to be an important part of the Dineen experience.

The streets of the subdivision were named for various holidays. The Dineens' trilevel was on Memorial Day Lane, and every parking space near it was taken. I was shown into the house by a son-in-law, Bill, and met another, Charlie, in the crowded front room. Their wives, Lynette and Leemarie, were seated on a sofa on either side of their mother, Louise. Three children, whose names I didn't catch, entered and exited the front room more or less continuously.

"I may sue the police," Louise informed me at the onset. She had shaved off her original eyebrows and substituted thin pencil lines, in the style of a 1930s movie star. She had a Hollywood tan as well and long fingernails whose blue enamel sparkled. "I think I have a good case."

She paused for my opinion, converting her assertion into a question. I asked a question of my own, one that might have been seen as a criticism of her "good case": Why had she told the police that her husband had taken off for parts unknown?

"That's all Doug ever talked about. When I met him thirty years ago, he told me I'd be moving around a lot if I married him. We went to school together, right down the road at Southport High. We planned to move to Phoenix after the wedding, but I found out I was carrying Lynette, so we couldn't go. When Lynette was old enough, Doug was talking about Boulder, Colorado, but then Leemarie came along. Then his folks got sick and then mine did and the kids were in school with all their friends and we didn't want to take them out. After the girls got married, Doug was all excited about Portland or Seattle, but Bill got laid off and he and Lynette and the kids moved in with us."

The daughters and their husbands then contributed their memories of places Dineen had talked of moving to or visiting. The list was like the index of an atlas. Eventually, Louise lost patience with this and took the floor again.

"When Dr. Meyers gave Bill the news about the spot on his lung, he said he wanted to run more tests right away. Doug put him off and went into work the next day like nothing had happened. I went to pick him up that night like always, and he was gone. Nobody saw him leave. He never came home after that or showed up at work. I figured he'd lit out for one of those places he'd talked about or maybe all of them. Who wouldn't of thought that?

"The police asked if any of his clothes were gone or any money. I told them just the clothes Doug was wearing and the money in his pocket. They thought he might be hitchhiking and working odd jobs for food. You can ask Leemarie, she heard them say it."

Leemarie nodded vigorously to confirm what appeared to be the linchpin of the family's legal campaign. I asked about the reported sighting of Dineen in Santa Fe, and Louise took it as another criticism, saying that she'd never put much stock in it and had only passed it on to the police out of a sense of duty.

I asked next if anyone had a theory as to why Dineen hadn't hitchhiked to the edge of the map as believed, why he'd chosen instead to go into that field. The result was silence. That is, the assembled adults were silent. In the next room, one of the children was beating on a pot with a wooden spoon and another was complimenting his technique. I listened to a minute or so of the recital and then took my leave.

I headed east on Southport Road toward I-65 and the office. Then I had a vision of Boxleiter asking me the last question I'd put to the Dineens. And I knew the resulting silence would be even more awkward than the one I'd just sat though, since I wouldn't have a kid with a pot and a spoon to provide useful cover. So I drove on past the ramp for the interstate and again made the hard left for the Home Station.

Once at the mall, I drove around back to the service road and let my Chevy inch forward at idle, past a row of back doors and Dumpsters. When I reached the end of the road, I parked and got out.

The doorway in which I spoken to Joseph Albini was still standing open. As I approached, someone stepped into it, drawing a cigarette from a pack as he moved from the interior gloom into the late afternoon light. It wasn't the ghost of Douglas Dineen. It was the first person I'd spoken to at the store, my one-time guide, Grady.

"I was hoping to see you again," he said. He put his unlit cigarette behind one ear and dusted one hand against the other. "I knew you weren't happy with that story I told you about Trigger. No, I could tell. You thought I was being disrespectful to old Doug by comparing him to a dog.

"I sure didn't mean it in a bad or a demeaning way. It's just that Doug's situation got me thinking again about Trigger's last day. It's something I've thought about a lot over the years. Why that dog did what he did, I mean. It took me a long time to come up with an answer."

Just then any answer sounded good to me. So I asked Grady why his dog had gone into that field alone. He retrieved his cigarette and lit it as he organized his thoughts.

"It was a puzzle for sure. Why would an animal that had hung at my heels all his life, done any dumb trick I'd asked him to, looked after my family and my house, just walk away from us when he needed us most? I wondered if some instinct might have told him that the end was coming. That same instinct could have canceled all bets somehow, maybe by awakening something locked in Trigger's genes, some memory of a time when dogs were free.

"If that was true, then in the last few moments of its life, thousand years of servitude to us, to men, might have been washed away. A dog suddenly freed of those chains would turn its back on sidewalks and mowed grass. It would look for whatever primeval patch it could find—even an old soybean field—and it would go alone. Like Trigger did."

Grady left me then, after another apology over "disrespecting" Dineen's death. I'd long since absolved him of the charge.

I walked out into Dineen's patch of the primeval and stood near the corner set off by yellow tape, wondering over the chains broken by Dineen's knowledge of impending death and of the thousands of years of civilization washed clean.

The afternoon rush hour was heating up, to judge by the steady rumble coming from the interstate. Above me, a breeze playing in the high-voltage wires contributed a shriller, singsong note.

I closed my eyes and listened. And by and by I heard waves breaking on a tropical beach.

FORGET ME NEVER

"You've been wanting to do an article on those damn roadside memorials," Boxleiter said. "Here's your big chance."

E.N. Boxleiter was my longtime editor at the *Star Republic*, the Indianapolis newspaper where I spent my days and many of my nights, and I'd learned to give his big chances a very critical examination, kicking their tires and looking into their mouths both. Not that it ever did me much good in the end.

Take the current example. As it happened, I had wanted to do a story on roadside memorials set up for accident victims, the homemade shrines that had become a common sight around Indiana. The memorials were the heart's work of some loving survivor of a person killed in a car or truck or motorcycle accident, and the earliest ones—the ones I'd first noticed—had been simple wooden crosses wired to a guardrail or mile marker or just stuck in the grass of a berm. Over the years the designs had evolved like the Christmas light displays of competitive neighbors. Now they commonly featured plastic wreaths, stuffed animals, and photos of the deceased.

I was never able to pass one without wondering about the phenomenon. Specifically, I always asked myself why the spot where a loved one had met a violent end seemed to be so much more meaningful to some industrious mourner than the victim's grave, the more traditional focal point of grief.

I'd gone as far as contacting a friend who taught cultural anthropology at Lockerbie University, a local private college. She'd told me of antecedents to the memorials that went all the way back to the Middle Ages, when it had been a common practice to erect roadside shrines for travelers killed by bandits. And she'd shared her pet theory that the roots of the practice were sunk even deeper. Despite the cross motif, she believed the shrines might spring from some racial memory of a time before the Christian concept of heaven became established. That explained to her satisfaction the focus on the site of death rather than the grave. It had been the last known whereabouts on earth of the dearly departed's spirit and therefore a likely spot for that spirit to hang around.

All of which might have made for an interesting feature article, if my editor had been interested in a simple feature. From me at least, Boxleiter expected something more offbeat. Something bizarre or with a scent of mystery. And now his pleased expression told me he had caught a whiff of that scent.

"Take a look," he said, pushing a Polaroid snapshot across his desk. He was holding four others with their backs to me, like a gambler stretching out a pat hand.

The photograph on the desktop was a close-up of a pretty typical roadside shrine: a white cross with a framed portrait attached to its intersection. The photo within the photo appeared to be of a smiling young woman, but it was very small. Above it, stick-on letters of the type used on mailboxes spelled the name Maria. A vase containing flowers was wired to the bottom of the cross.

Because I could see that the prints my boss still held each had a notation on the back, I turned over the one he'd dealt me. In smudged felt tip was written "I-70 westbound near the 94 mile marker."

I waited for the punch line, and Boxleiter laid the other photos down, almost reluctantly. I thought at first that they were four different shots of the same memorial. Each showed a white cross bearing the name Maria, the same framed black-and-white photo, and the same glass vase. Each vase contained the same bouquet. The slight differences in the lighting of each shot could have been due to their having been taken at different times of day. But then I noticed some significant variations in the backgrounds. The mile post just visible in the original photo didn't appear in any of the four near duplicates. And one of the four clearly showed a bit of guardrail where there shouldn't have been any.

To confirm the likeliest explanation, I checked the backs of prints. Sure enough, each had a different location smeared there. One was I-70 eastbound at the 94 mile marker, putting its shrine right across four lanes of interstate from the one I'd first examined. Another was Shadeland Avenue at Tenth Street. The remaining two were I-65 southbound near the Keystone exit and I-465, Indy's beltway, westbound near the exit for State Road 67, on the city's southwest side.

Boxleiter was nodding. "Exactly. Five identical memorials to a woman identified only by her first name. The Polaroids were taken by a highway maintenance guy named Halleck. He noticed the two on I-70 because that's on his normal grass cutting route. They got him so interested, he talked them up back at the highway garage and another grass cutter mentioned the one on I-465. After that, Halleck spent a Saturday afternoon driving around town. He found the other crosses, photographed them, and sent us the results.

"He's a man after my own heart, this Halleck," Boxleiter concluded. "He wants an explanation. So do I."

I reached Halleck, first name Alan, in the cab of his tractor, thanks to the miracle of cellular communications. He agreed to meet me at the first cross he'd found, the one on I-70 westbound at the 94 mile marker.

On my drive from downtown, I used my own cell phone to reach my friend the Lockerbie cultural anthropologist.

Professor Constance Brewster—Connie when we'd been undergraduates together—was about to leave for a lecture. I gave her a quick description of the mystery shrines and asked for a quick opinion.

"Fakes obviously," she said in her decisive way. "The question is, why would anyone bother? You say these memorials are basically big white crosses? That's interesting. You know, ever since the courts started ruling against religious displays on public property—manger scenes, ten commandment plaques, or whatever—I've been expecting some kind of grass roots reaction. This could be an example of that. The highways are public land, after all. Some religious activist could be setting these up as a way of thumbing his nose at the court rulings. Who's going to tear down a memorial to an accident victim?"

I asked her why, if these were protests, they all featured the same photo and name.

"Why not?" Connie asked back. "Maybe it's to make them recognizable to the faithful. Wait a minute, you said the name was Maria? Could that photograph have been a picture of the Virgin Mary? They can do some amazing things with graphics programs these days. It could be Our Lady of Czestochowa with Cindy Crawford's hair pasted on. Check it out and get back to me."

Alan Halleck's mowing rig was parked on the shoulder of the interstate when I arrived. I pulled well onto the grass myself, but I still felt my car shake as a semi rumbled past.

"You get used to that," Halleck said when I finally ventured outside the car. "The crazy traffic. It's like working around a big buzz saw or in a fireworks factory. You have to put the danger out of your mind or you can't do your job."

Halleck was a young, muscular guy dressed in work boots, khaki shorts, and a green YMCA shirt. He was tanned enough to make a dermatologist cry, though his eyes were well protected by mirrored sunglasses that would not have looked out of place in a Ferrari. The shades were hooked behind ears that might have won him the nickname Jughead in a less sensitive time and supported by a square, flat nose. His sun-lightened hair was also square, his flattop as perfectly manicured as any country club green.

"There's another occupational hazard," he said, pointing to the shrine to the mysterious Maria. "You can't just mow over them. I mean, you could, but it wouldn't seem right. I mow around them until the grass gets too high. Then I stop, pull them out, mow, and stick them back in. A real pain."

The cross was taller than I'd judged from the Polaroid, almost four feet high. The picture at its center, which was enclosed in a dime-store frame, was a five by seven. The print's quality was so poor that it might have been done on a Xerox machine, but it didn't appear to have been altered or doctored in any way. It certainly didn't resemble any image of the Blessed Virgin I'd ever seen. That it could have been a high school graduation picture was suggested by the subject's age and the appealing openness of her smile and her wide dark eyes.

"I might never have noticed the duplication if I hadn't taken the time to trim around this one," Halleck was saying. "They all look a little alike, these cross things. But the picture of the girl caught my eye. She's a real cutie. A Mexican beauty, as the song says. It'd be a shame if she was really dead."

I asked Halleck why he thought she might not be.

"It's got to be a fake, right? You can't die in five different places; I don't care how bad the wreck is. When I finally got around to noticing that there was an identical cross on the other side"—he pointed toward the eastbound lanes, which were cut off from view at that point by a grove of trees—"I thought, okay, she died on the median and the trees make that a bad place for a memorial, so her family put one on both sides. Or maybe her papa uses this road to commute and he wanted to remember her coming and going.

"But then I mentioned them to Bud Bishop, who mows down on I-465, and he told me about the one down there. He'd gotten a little sweet on Maria himself, seeing her picture every couple of weeks. That started me hunting around. By the time I found the fifth cross, I knew something else was going on."

A little convoy of trucks passed just then, interrupting Halleck. Or giving him the perfect opportunity to pause for added effect. I could tell he had a theory he was dying to impart. When the truck noise died away, I asked him about it.

He removed his sunglasses, revealing blue eyes surrounded by relatively undamaged skin. "I think little Maria's got herself a stalker. I think some guy who's hot for her, maybe some guy she's dumped, is setting these things up where he knows she'll see them. Like threats, you know. Come back to me or it's RIP. The trouble is, the jerk didn't blow the photo up big enough. They're so small you can't really make out the face from the highway. Maria could be driving past them every day and still not know the danger she's in.

"What you have to do is run Maria's picture in the paper. Get her to come forward so we can talk to her. Warn her, I mean."

I noted the "we" and wondered if Maria might be well on her way to having a second stalker. I knew how Boxleiter would react to the idea of running a dating service, so I took the conversation in a new direction by asking Halleck when the white crosses had first appeared.

"Not all that long ago. This one wasn't here back in the early spring when I was having to cut this stretch every week. And then I cut around it for a while before I climbed down that first time to move it. So it might have been put out four weeks or so ago. Around the end of June."

Even that vague date would be useful in identifying the fatal accident, assuming, as I did, that Halleck's stalker theory was wishful thinking. He gave it another try after I'd thanked him and told him I'd be in touch.

"Take a good look at that picture. That's a girl men fall in love with. If you talk to her, remember I saw her first."

I was on my way back downtown to sift through accident reports when I decided instead to get off the highway at Shadeland Avenue and visit the only shrine to Maria that wasn't on an interstate. Not that I saw any significance in that. I was only looking for the visit to delay some tedious desk work. As it turned out, it eliminated that step completely.

The Shadeland cross was stuck in a weedy island of grass that divided the avenue's three badly paved northbound lanes from its three equally cracked southbound lanes. I parked on the apron of a defunct Shell station and approached the cross on foot. Even before I'd reached the safety of the median, I could tell that Halleck's photo hadn't lied. This shrine was an exact duplicate of the one I'd just left, right down to the bouquet of white plastic flowers in its vase.

I was trying, idly, to identify those flowers when a police siren, blaring out behind me, almost shot me into the northbound traffic. Then a Marion County sheriff's department cruiser slid to a halt beside me, every light flashing.

The woman who climbed out was in such a hurry she

had trouble settling her Canadian-Mountie-style hat on her head. "Hold it!" she shouted, and then, "Damn."

The last comment was a sign of recognition. Like most reporters, I knew my share of policemen and women. I knew Deputy Sheila Gilkey all too well. She was an avid marathon runner whose opinion of the press was even lower than her percentage of body fat.

"I should have known you'd sniff this out sooner or later," she said.

I accepted the compliment graciously, not mentioning all the sniffing done for me by Alan Halleck. I was thinking that Gilkey knew all about Halleck, that he'd sent a duplicate set of his Polaroids to the Sheriff's Department. The question she asked next told me this wasn't the case.

"Who's onto this besides me and you?"

I told her the *Star Republic* had been tipped by an alert reader and showed her the five photos. She examined them at length, ignoring the traffic backup created by her parked cruiser.

"Your nosy reader missed one," she finally said. "On Post Road just south of Pendleton Pike. It was the first one I saw. I'd been going out there almost every day on one of my regular cases." Gilkey worked in the county's domestic violence unit. "I had every inch of that route memorized, including a white cross with Maria printed on it. Then I'm down on the south side near 67, on my way to take a deposition, and I see an identical cross on I-465. Couldn't believe my eyes. Had to drive back up to Post Road to make sure the original one was still there."

She went on to explain what I'd already guessed: She'd made an off-duty tour of the city, searching for other white crosses. It was surprising that she and Halleck hadn't crossed paths.

"Have you IDed her?" Gilkey asked, pushing her Mountie hat back to reveal a little of the bowl-cut brown hair that matched the brown of her uniform shirt so exactly she might have been dying it to departmental specs. I could tell by the look in her slightly protruding eyes—also regulation brown—that she had identified Maria. I could also tell that she was dying to tell someone, even a troublesome reporter. And I understood that. The more interesting the story, the greater the pressure to give it away.

"Her name is Maria Felez," Gilkey said. "I won't tell you how many of my free evenings that cost me. I spent them going through accident reports looking for Marias and then tracking down photographs. It was a break from dealing with molesters and abusers, anyway."

She made it sound like one of Hercules's tougher assignments. I asked her how many Marias could possibly have been killed last spring.

"Last spring? Maria died in 1997."

Five years earlier. My next dumb question involved the crosses themselves. I asked which of the half dozen actually marked the site of Maria's accident.

"None of them. She was killed out on the west side. She was a senior at Ben Davis High School out there. I found her picture in the Ben Davis yearbook." She pointed to the frame on the cross. "That very one. A couple of weeks after her graduation she was T-boned by a drunk driver at the intersection of Girls School Road and Tenth Street.

"I'll save you a drive out there. There's no cross at the intersection. No nothing. And here's something else to chew on. Her family moved away right after she died. They hadn't been in Indy very long when it happened and they decided they didn't like the place. Can't say I blame them.

"I spoke with her father, who's out in Phoenix now. Nice guy. He said he didn't know anything about any memorials. The only person he could think of who might be putting them up is a boyfriend she had at Ben Davis. Mr. Felez couldn't recall the kid's name, but he did remember that he didn't like him. Said he was into gangs."

She paused to let that detail sink in so long it got all the way to my shoes. I asked the question she was obviously waiting for: What did gangs have to do with the crosses?

Gilkey said, "I think these memorials may be some kind of gang sign. See those white flowers? When I first found these things, they all had pink flowers hanging on them. Identical plastic bouquets. Then overnight they all were switched to red flowers. Now they're all suddenly white. Why? Why change plastic flowers at all? I think it's some kind of code. Some of the gangs are into drug smuggling. The different colors may be advertisements for different shipments or a way of letting couriers know it's safe to come in.

"I think Maria's old boyfriend dreamt it up. Maybe he's still sentimental about her or maybe he just had her picture handy. What do you think?"

I thought that Deputy Gilkey needed a break from domestic violence cases so badly she'd created a new assignment for herself out of fairly thin air. But I didn't say that. I asked instead why she had been staking out the Shadeland cross.

"It's the closest one to my apartment. I'm keeping watch on my own time. If I can catch the guy who's changing the flowers, I can find out what this is all about. I thought I'd caught him just now. Instead. . ."

She'd caught a reporter. Now that the impulse to tell her story had been satisfied, she was regretting giving in to it.

"Listen. What I told you just now is off the record. I mean, it's part of an ongoing investigation."

Neither of those claims had much going for it. Before she could invoke attorney client privilege or the seal of the confessional, I promised her I wouldn't write anything about gangs or drug shipments.

This time I headed downtown and actually made it. At the newspaper's offices, I bypassed my desk and went straight to the library—formerly the morgue—where back issues of the *Star Republic* were kept, some on newsprint, some on microfiche, and some on disk. I asked a librarian named

Glenda to do a computer search on Maria Felez. After killing two minutes telling me how I could be doing the search myself at my own terminal at my own desk, Glenda typed a few keystrokes and printed off three articles from three different 1997 editions of the paper.

The first described Maria's fatal accident. The second was the girl's very short obituary, which had been supplemented by her yearbook photo. The third article, the one I was really after, reported that the drunk driver who'd killed her, a twenty-five-year-old mechanic named Wallace Ristine, had pled guilty to vehicular homicide and been sentenced to ten years.

What had gotten me thinking of Maria's killer was a discrepancy between Alan Halleck's story and Deputy Gilkey's. The deputy had told me that Maria had been killed five years earlier, but Halleck had been certain that the memorial crosses hadn't appeared until June. Why the five-year gap? If Gilkey was right and the shrines were gang alerts dreamt up by Maria's old boyfriend, the gap wasn't hard to explain. The boyfriend simply hadn't needed the scheme or thought of it until last June. But another, likelier explanation was that the designer and builder of the shrines had spent the five years between Maria's death and the appearance of her memorials behind bars.

I called a contact in the Indiana Department of Corrections, and he confirmed that Ristine had been released in early June, after his sentence had been halved for good behavior. My informant was more reluctant to share Ristine's current address, but in the end he did. The ex-con had an apartment on Post Road, not far from the first cross Sheila Gilkey had noticed.

I drove out to Post and established that Ristine wasn't at home. Then I had what was either a late lunch or an early dinner. Following that, I settled in to wait.

The man I was after showed up around four. He was overweight and seemed to carry the bulk of the load below his waist, but that impression might have been the work of his outfit: baggy tan coveralls with the logo of a motor oil company displayed on the back. Ristine's red hair was thinning and his skin was very pale. I had the feeling it would have been just as pale no matter where he'd spent the last five years.

He turned when I said his name, and I saw that he was trying to grow the kind of goatee then called a "soul patch." His eyes were very tired, which, like his pallor, may or may not have been a temporary condition.

"What do you want?" he asked.

I wanted an interview. I decided the best way to get one was to jump right in. So I showed him my press card and asked him why he was setting up shrines all over town to the woman he'd killed.

He blinked twice and then corrected me. "Not all over town. Just on the routes I'm allowed to drive. I'm still on a restricted license. I can only drive to and from my job and to visit my mom and my sister. I work at a truck stop out east on Mount Comfort Road. My mom's in a place just off Shadeland. My sister lives down on Kentucky Avenue."

Otherwise known as State Road 67. That accounted for all the crosses. Ristine had volunteered a lot of information. People often did that when they didn't want to answer the one question put to them. I repeated my unanswered question for the mechanic, just in case he'd forgotten it.

"Why am I doing it?" He passed his tongue over his lips. "Come inside and I'll tell you."

He led me into a second-floor efficiency whose plaid furniture and imitation oil paintings were surely also rented. Spread out on a dinette table were the makings of more Maria shrines: lengths of wood, white paint, frames, vases, sheets of reflective letters. Ristine hurried past the supplies, opened the refrigerator door, and took out a sixteen-ounce bottle of Coke. He drank half of it off, and it seemed to steady him.

"I'm an alcoholic," he said.

I thought he was dodging my question again, but he wasn't.

"Right now, right this minute, I'm dying for a drink. After killing someone and spending five years in prison for it, I still want one. I've tried everything to make it go away, but it never has. I can't go an hour without thinking about it. I can't get into a car without wanting to drive to a bar or a liquor store.

"The only thing that stops me from taking a drink is thinking about Maria, the girl I killed." He drained the Coke bottle and hurriedly added. "What I'm saying is, I never want to hurt anybody again.

"Thinking about Maria—about how I took an innocent life—helps me, but it got so it wasn't enough. One day I noticed this wreath of flowers somebody had set up by the side of the road, and I thought, 'Maria should have one of those.' The next thing I knew, I was making one. And then another and another. I put them up on my normal routes, at spots where I caught myself thinking about a beer. I look up now and I see the white cross and her picture and I don't want the drink.

"That's the whole sick story. I'm sorry if you were looking for something more, but that's the big secret. Just a lousy drunk trying to stay dry."

Not a religious protester or a mad stalker or a gang leader with a penchant for floral codes. All those stories had been wrong. But I decided, watching Ristine try to suck more cola from his empty bottle, that his story was wrong, too. Or at least incomplete.

For one thing, it didn't explain the characteristic of the shrines that had so fascinated Deputy Gilkey. I asked Ristine why, if the shrines were just reminders not to drink, he changed the artificial flowers so regularly. He licked his lips again and said nothing.

Playing a hunch, I asked him if he'd mind showing me his

wallet. He stared at me for a long time, his pale skin looking even more like the shaded side of a fish. Then he took out the wallet, opened it up, and handed it over.

He'd opened it to display a clear plastic sleeve intended to protect a photograph. Behind the plastic was Maria Felez's yearbook photo, cut from the pages of the *Star Republic*. I'd encountered the portrait over and over again, but this was by far the clearest print I'd seen. She really had been a beautiful girl, bursting with the hope and happiness that made most people her age attractive. But there was something more to her beauty than just youth and a nice smile. It was the promise in those dark eyes of a person as beautiful as the face.

"I cut that out of the paper," Ristine said. "I don't know why. Should have been the last face I ever wanted to see. When I was inside, I had it on the wall of my cell. The other guys thought she was my girl, and I let them think it. After a while, I started believing it myself. Why not? Her life was over and so was mine. Wasn't like either of us was ever going to have anybody else."

Maria was a woman men fell in love with, Halleck had said. It was certainly true for Wallace Ristine. I handed back his wallet. Then I reminded him that his life wasn't over. And I said that I couldn't believe Maria Felez would want him throwing away all the years he had left.

He was shaking his head before I'd finished. "I'm not throwing anything away. I'm atoning. Who knows? Maria and I may meet again someday. May really meet. I want to be ready. If there's just one chance in a million, I want to be ready."

THE COMPLETE WORKS OF FRANZ DREISMAN

————

I was told the story of Franz Dreisman by Professor Carla Higham of Lockerbie University, a small college on the near north side of Indianapolis. During my days at Lockerbie, Higham had been my favorite English instructor, but I hadn't seen her from the day of my graduation until one evening some two years later when I bumped into her on the Lockerbie campus. I was a cub reporter by then, working for the local daily, the *Star Republic*. I was researching a story on the university's new fitness center, an assignment that made any distraction welcome. Higham seemed to be in the same frame of mind. When I asked her how the Wordsworth business was going, she shook her head sadly. "Daffodils before swine," she said.

She took me by the elbow and walked me across College

Avenue to a small bar. The neon sign above the door said "Assignations," but Higham called it the faculty lounge. She hadn't changed very much since my undergraduate days. Her wavy shoulder length hair was a little grayer and her always narrow-eyed expression was now nearly a squint, but her plaid dress and cashmere cardigan seemed very familiar, as did her penchant for flashy, oversized costume jewelry.

Between sips of wine and to the accompaniment of the jingling of her several bracelets, Higham reminisced indiscreetly about old campus scandals. We arrived at Franz Dreisman's tale by way of misappropriated funds, several divorces, and a sex change operation. When she finally spoke of Dreisman, Higham's face lost its look of amused detachment. I found myself leaning forward in my chair, making an effort to hear her oddly quiet voice.

● ● ●

This happened (said Professor Higham) before your time at Lockerbie. Though even if you'd been a student then, you might not have heard of Dreisman. He wasn't a well-known person around the campus. No, by no means. He was really very little known, considering the length of his tenure. Dreisman was a lay teacher of Theology, a rare thing in those days and not common now, God help us.

I met him shortly after my first husband passed away. Dreisman was a widower. I spent many a long evening at his apartment, talking things out. It was on Meridian around

Thirtieth Street, an old flat with twelve-foot ceilings and a huge fireplace. His wife, dead years before I met him, had been an art instructor and an enthusiastic collector. There was some money on her side of the family, and she had turned that apartment into a small art gallery. By the time I saw the place, the paintings were the only sign of her left.

Like many widowed men, Dreisman had reverted to his bachelor ways, which were, to put it kindly, careless. I remember always having to clear a space before I could sit down, before I could even move. The floors were carpeted with old newspapers, the tables held stacks of dirty dishes, and the dusty chairs were piled with dustier books. His wife's collection had been similarly neglected. Dreisman, out of some feeling for his wife I suppose, would allow no one to touch the paintings, but he was too lazy to even straighten them himself. The finest piece of the collection, a small oil of the Madonna and Child, by a Belgian named Gileste I think, hung at an absurd angle. The Babe seemed ready to tumble from the frame at any moment.

Dreisman was a reflection of his apartment, though of course it was the other way around. His gray hair was always unkempt, his clothes slept in. His hands were finely shaped, but they were stained with ink and nicotine and the nails were long and yellow. Now, I'm not trying to say that Dreisman was a bad man, because he really wasn't. He was a dedicated scholar and a thoughtful friend. His dishevelment was merely superficial, as he often told me, but I've always been a careful dresser myself, and it bothered me. During my visits I'd chide him on the subject. More often than I should have, God rest his soul.

He was, as I've said, a good man, but he'd developed a rather odd idea. I knew that he'd been deeply affected by his wife's death, and when he was told that he was going to die soon himself, well, I think it was too much for his mind. He told me about his terminal illness quite calmly one day while we were discussing a film. He wasn't worried about it, you see, because of his idea.

I really should tell you something about his work first. His final treatise, the work of his last two or three years, was on one of the apocryphal books of the New Testament. These were writings rejected by the early Christian Church and not included in the canon of any subsequent sect. Dreisman's subject was the Acts of Pilate, in which Christ's decent into hell following His crucifixion is described. Outside my field, but damned interesting.

Now, back to Dreisman's strange idea. He had decided that this work of his was important, important to God. So important, that he would be spared to complete it. We all write personal corollaries to the standard rules of our religions. Those of us who still have religions. Dreisman just took a common idea, that we're all here on earth for a purpose, and carried it to an egotistical extreme. His single justifying act was to be a great act. It was given to Franz

Dreisman to die, like Nelson at Trafalgar, at the height of his accomplishments.

Dreisman gave me his fullest explanation of the idea on that last day. I had made the mistake of mentioning both free will and dirty dishes in the same conversation, and he was rather irritated.

"To speak of an individual will is pointless," he told me. "Your will, Carla Higham's will, is as inconsequential as Carla Higham's plan for the universe. You have no plan. You couldn't possibly begin to conceive of the enormity of the universe, never mind try to shape its destiny."

"You're spilling coffee on your robe," I said.

"Listen to me," Dreisman said. "We're tools, like Abraham and Moses and Paul were tools. God forged each of us specially for our tasks. He works through us. He uses our talents, just as we use our hammers and saws and typewriters—"

"And vacuum cleaners," I interjected.

"Be quiet!" Dreisman commanded. "God needs us no less for having created us. We cannot live without our tools merely because we invented them. On the contrary, we grow more dependent on them every day. I am not important in God's eye, not in myself, no more important than anyone else, but because my task is important, because it is significant, I know I will be spared to complete it."

"Please don't bang your fist," I said. "The dust is choking me."

He settled back in his chair and smiled. "It's intoxicating, really, this idea. I have to fight against a feeling of pride. I thank God for this illness of mine, I really do. It made it all clear to me, made me see, made me get back to work. I might have lived another fifteen years, lecturing to those students, those religious deaf mutes. Might never have seen that I was a link in a chain. An immortal chain. . ."

He dropped off to sleep then as he often did. His medication, I think. That day, instead of quietly taking my leave, I decided to straighten up just a bit. It didn't seem right for a sick man to be living in that sty. I started with the sofa, piling books in one corner and old newspapers by the door. I was getting down to the sofa itself when I happened upon what must once have been a corned beef sandwich, tucked in the folds of a three-month-old copy of the *Star Republic*. I don't remember whether I cried out in disgust, but I did toss the newspaper and decomposing sandwich across the room, knocking a week's worth of dirty glasses off the coffee table. Reflexes, I suppose.

Dreisman sat bolt upright. "What in God's name are you doing?" he yelled at me. "What are you doing?"

Now, this man had been kind to me and he was sick and maybe a little crazy, but I had had enough. I was sarcastic.

"I was trying to find your apartment," I yelled back. "I think it's buried here somewhere."

"What are you doing?" Dreisman repeated, not quite awake.

"I was straightening up, Franz. Look at this place. Do you think that any work you have to do is important enough for you to be rooting around in garbage like an animal? What do you think your wife would say if she could see you? It would break her heart. Look at her beautiful paintings. Look at them. They're falling off the walls."

"That's enough!" Dreisman shouted, thoroughly enraged. "I see now I'll never convince you that I haven't time left for these petty concerns."

He rose from his seat, kicked his way through the scattered papers to the far wall, and took the Gileste painting, the tilting Madonna and Child, by the frame.

"I hope this will satisfy you," he said over his shoulder. With that he straightened the painting with one swift movement.

He took a slow step backward. I thought he was admiring the work, but when he turned toward me I saw that his face had paled and his hand was over his heart. At first he looked confused. Then, over the course of perhaps a minute, a thin smile spread across his face. Still open-eyed, he fell forward onto the floor. The cloud of dust he created rose almost to the ceiling.

• • •

Higham sat for a long time, staring down at the table between us.

"Poor Dreisman," she said at last. "It was a shame about

his manuscript. No one was able to make sense of it. He was so sure that God would spare him to complete it. If I've made him appear foolish, I apologize, because he wasn't that. He was simply a poor, mistaken man."

I stood up and said goodnight to Higham. Outside the air was cold and the sky was black and enormous. I felt like a man standing in the bottom of a deep pit. I'd had an odd idea of my own while listening to the account of Dreisman's death. I hadn't mentioned it to Higham, but it stayed with me all the way home. What if God had spared Dreisman to complete his task after all? What if Dreisman had simply exaggerated his role and underestimated his Creator's attention to detail?

I forgot all about the new Lockerbie fitness center that night. Instead I wrote the story of Franz Dreisman, his last act, and that thin smile of understanding. The next morning, I gave it to my editor, E.N. Boxleiter. I didn't think he would print it, and I was right.

But he did smile his own thin smile as he dropped the pages into the wastebasket by his desk. "Who knows?" he said. "Maybe I'm saving your life."

About the Author

Terence Faherty is the author of the romantic Irish mystery *The Quiet Woman* as well as the Edgar-nominated Owen Keane series, which follows the adventures of a failed seminarian turned metaphysical detective, and the Shamus-winning Scott Elliott private eye series, which is set in the golden age of Hollywood. His short fiction has won the Macavity Award from Mystery Readers International.

Terry lives in Indianapolis, Indiana, with his wife Jan.

www.ingramcontent.com/pod-product-compliance
Lightning Source LLC
Chambersburg PA
CBHW020638110726
47899CB00002B/817